Sunshine

Over Snow

Logan and Roxy
Summer Lake Seasons Book Three

By SJ McCoy

A Sweet n Steamy Romance

Published by Xenion, Inc

Published by Xenion, Inc.
First paperback edition 2019
www.sjmccoy.com

Cover Design by Dana Lamothe of Designs by Dana
Editor: Mitzi Pummer Carroll
Proofreaders: Aileen Blomberg, Marisa Nichols, Traci Atkinson.

ISBN: 978-1-946220-59-2

Dedication

For Denise.

You'll know why.

Love you, my friend.

J

oxo

Chapter One

"Reel your tongue back in, would you, Josh? If you can't drag your eyes away from those chicks and focus on what's going on here, we're going to have to take our team-building lunches back on site."

Josh shook his head as if to clear it and gave Logan a rueful smile. "Sorry, boss, but come on. I mean ... look at them. You're not telling me you wouldn't?"

Aaron laughed. "That's not the point. We all know he would. But not on work time."

Logan smiled. "Exactly. I'm not blaming you for being interested. I am, too, especially in the little redhead. My point is that they'll still be around once the workday is done. Work is work and play is play—ne'er the twain shall meet. Come five o'clock this afternoon, it's a different matter. We can probably get them over to the Boathouse this evening, and that'll be time enough to play."

"Right now, this lunch is about us hanging out together off-site so we can talk about what's going on." He chuckled. "We're here to bond with each other as a team—you have to save your attempts at bonding with a pretty lady for later."

The redhead caught his eye and smiled. He smiled back. He got the impression she'd be up for whatever kind of bonding he suggested—but he'd have to save it for later, just the same as Josh.

"So, tell me what's going on? What snags have we hit this week, and what do we need to set up ready for next week?"

The crew forgot about the girls sitting on the other side of the café as they took turns to share their progress and detail the problems they'd hit and the resources they needed going forward.

Logan loved these Friday lunches. Phase four of the development here at Four Mile Creek was starting to take shape. He loved his job as construction manager, and over the last couple of years, he'd managed to shape the crew into an effective team who got stuff done. These lunches had been a part of that. The guys gave him shit for throwing around phrases like bonding and team-building, and he let them—they didn't like to look at it that way, but the truth was that it had worked. He'd been brought in to pull the project together; it'd been behind schedule with all kinds of problems. It hadn't taken long to see that they all stemmed back to a horrible working environment. Now, instead of warring factions who blamed each other for any problems that arose, he had a crew made up of different teams who all understood the part they played in the big picture and pulled together to do their part.

He looked up when Brian, his scheduling manager, came into the café and cursed under his breath when Brian stopped to chat with the girls Josh had been ogling earlier. They only waylaid him for a few moments, but it was long enough to derail the meeting again.

Josh winked at Logan. "You can bet your ass they'll be coming over to the Boathouse tonight. Brian doesn't waste time. He could charm the panties off a nun."

Brian grinned as he reached the table and overheard them. He slapped the back of Josh's head. "You're right; they said they'll come to the Boathouse tonight. But even I don't work that fast. I'd talked to the blonde one in town earlier, said I might see her over here."

Logan sighed. The other guys were glancing over at the girls again; he doubted he'd be able to get them to refocus on work. It didn't matter, they'd done all they needed to. He knew what he needed to work on this afternoon to smooth as many wrinkles out of next week as he could.

Brian smiled at him. "You'll be out tonight, right?"

"I sure will. It's Friday. Time to let loose."

"And find yourself a loose woman?"

Logan grinned. "That's right."

"Damn!" They all followed Josh's gaze to the plaza outside, where a woman was hurrying her way toward the café.

Logan reconsidered his choice of the redhead when he spotted this one. She was a little taller, long brown hair, pretty face, but it was the way she bounced her way across the terrace that really sucked him in. They were full; big, but bouncy. Maybe they weren't real? He smiled. He wasn't picky. He wouldn't turn down the chance to find out.

She came inside and went straight to the girls at the table. He should have known. She looked like she fit right in with them. They were all kind of preppy looking—from money, by the looks of them.

"Oh my God, girls! You'll never guess who I just ran into!" Logan cringed. Her voice had the same effect on him as nails on a blackboard. It was high and nasally, and … he shuddered. Not even that beautiful rack was worth enduring that sound for.

He glanced around the table. It seemed all the guys were waiting, just like he was, to hear who she'd just run into.

"Who?" asked the redhead.

"Roxy!"

"Roxy Buchanon?"

"Yep. Can you believe it? She lives here. She works on the front desk at the lodge."

"Awkward!" exclaimed the blonde.

The redhead made a face. "Not really. It's not as though she kept in touch either."

The blonde looked guilty. "She tried harder than I did. It's just …" She shrugged. "I feel bad that I didn't even invite her."

"Why would you? It's not as though she was ever really one of us."

"That's not fair," said the blonde. "She was."

The brunette with the big breasts shook her head. "No. She wasn't. We let her hang out with us, but she was only a scholarship kid. She wasn't even pretty. None of the guys were interested in her."

"But you had a crush on her brother," added the redhead with a laugh.

Logan unclenched his jaw when Josh gave him an inquiring look. "Roxy's a friend of yours, right?"

He nodded, surprised at how hard his heart was beating in his chest. He looked down and saw his hands curled into fists on the table. He was pissed. Those girls thought they were better than Roxy? They were full of it. She was worth more than all of them put together, any day of the week. Roxy was awesome.

He glanced back at the girls who were chattering and giggling, and his blood boiled. They'd better not be laughing about Roxy.

He turned when the café door opened, and she came in. His heart rate shot up again. It always did that when she came into a room. She was gorgeous, all long blonde hair and curves. If none of the boys at school or college or wherever she knew those girls from had been interested in her, they must have been blind. He'd love to get his hands on that body, but she was his friend.

He watched through narrowed eyes as she approached the girls' table, and they all turned fake smiles on her and got up and greeted her with squeals and air kisses. She looked genuinely pleased to see them, and that hurt him for her. She deserved better than that.

"It's so good to see you all!" She smiled around at them.

"And you," said the blonde. "I had no idea you lived here. And I'm sorry I didn't invite you."

Roxy let it go with a smile. "That's okay, we haven't talked in ages. I'm so pleased for you. Congratulations."

"Thanks." The blonde looked uncomfortable. "I'm afraid we've given them the final numbers for tomorrow night. I can't add you at this point."

"That's okay. I wouldn't expect you to."

"But we're going out tonight. We're going over to the other side of the lake, to someplace called the Boathouse. Do you know it? Would you want to come?"

Roxy smiled. "I'll be there."

The redhead glanced over at Logan and the guys and smiled. "We're making friends here already."

Roxy followed her gaze and smiled at them. Her smile faded a little when she looked at Logan. He hated that he seemed to have that effect on her. He got the feeling he pissed her off sometimes by just existing. He wasn't going to let it get to him today, though. He smiled back at her and got to his feet.

He hated seeing her standing there looking pleased to see those girls when he knew what they'd just been saying about her.

"Hey, Rox." He went to her side and put his arm around her shoulders.

The redhead's smile soured as she watched, and the brunette raised an eyebrow.

He was more concerned with Roxy's reaction. He joked around with all the girls in their group of friends, but he didn't often dare with Roxy. She was too swift to put him in his place. She surprised him by smiling up at him and leaning into his side, as though, for once, she was pleased to see him.

"Hey, you."

"I need to get the guys back to work, I'm guessing you need to get back yourself. But I just wanted to make sure that we're on for tonight?"

Her eyes widened a little, but she nodded. "Yeah. We are."

Logan wasn't sure that she understood what he was doing. He wasn't sure he totally understood it himself. He just wanted these bitchy, stuck-up girls to see that the boys were interested in Roxy now. He wanted to make them see—and to make her feel—that she was way better than any of them.

He couldn't resist it; he dropped a kiss on her forehead. "Go on, you'd better get back over there. I'll see you later."

Her cheeks flushed a little, and she nodded breathlessly. She was probably madder than hell at him for doing that. He'd hear about it later, no doubt. But at least it got her away from them and back to work. He didn't want her around them until he could tell her what they were really like.

She smiled at the girls. "He's right. I should get back. I'll see you at the Boathouse tonight."

Logan watched her leave and then turned back to the guys who were all watching him with puzzled looks on their faces. All except Aaron, who gave him an appreciative nod.

"What the fuck, dude?" asked Josh. "Why blow your chance with the redhead by making it look as though you're with Roxy? You know that's how that looked, right?"

Aaron laughed. "I believe that's why he did it. Roxy's a friend; those girls are nothing."

"I wouldn't say nothing," said Josh. "They're a potential score."

Logan shook his head sadly. "Josh, Josh, Josh. You have so much to learn. The kind of score you're talking about is worth next to nothing—cheap and easy. A friend is worth everything. And even if she weren't a friend, Roxy is worth more than all of those girls put together, and if you can't see that, there's no hope for you."

Josh blew out a sigh. "All right. I get it. It was kind of cool what you did there, actually. But I don't think it'll get you anywhere."

"I'm not trying to get anywhere. That's the whole point. Roxy's my friend."

Josh laughed. "Your friend who you've had the biggest crush on for longer than I can remember."

"I don't have a crush on her. At least, no more than any other woman. I like women. Especially beautiful ones. Roxy's beautiful." He shrugged.

Aaron held his gaze for a moment. "If you expect any of us to believe that …" His expression changed. "Or do *you* really believe that?"

"Believe it? Of course, I do. It's the truth."

Aaron chuckled. "Wow. There's none so blind …"

Logan shook his head. "You're the blind one. If I had a crush on Roxy, why wouldn't I have done something about it by now?"

Aaron shrugged. "You tell me, boss. You tell me."

Logan sat behind the wheel of the van he used to shuttle the guys over here from the work site and watched them get in. Aaron was nuts. Sure, he liked Roxy, but not like that. He pursed his lips. She was a friend. That was all.

Roxy was more than happy to get out of work once six o'clock rolled around. It'd been a long and busy week, and she had the whole weekend off for once. She usually worked at least Saturday or Sunday, often both. But the way the shifts had fallen, she had both days off. She pointed the car south down East Shore Road and headed home.

The timing couldn't be better. She'd hate to have to work this weekend. She couldn't believe her eyes when she'd seen Courtney strolling through reception earlier. And when she'd told her that all the girls were here for Lucy's hen weekend, she'd been surprised, to say the least. They'd been her group of friends in college. At least, they'd been the people she hung out with. She blew out a sigh. Lucy was the nicest of them, and Roxy had tried to keep in touch with her for a while, but it had become obvious that their friendship was one-sided, and she'd let it go. She'd decided after yet another unreturned call that she'd wait for Lucy to contact her—and that had been over two years ago.

Now they were here for the weekend, and Roxy was glad that she wouldn't be sitting on the front desk watching them come and go the whole time. If she knew them, there'd be an assortment of guys going back to their rooms with them over the weekend, and she wouldn't want to be the one to enforce the policy of having no unregistered guests staying over.

She might not have to see them at work, but she would run into them tonight. She imagined they'd be easy enough to avoid. They'd be all about hooking up. Hopefully, Lucy wouldn't—since she was the one getting married—maybe she'd want to hang with Roxy and catch up. That'd be okay. But other than that, Roxy guessed that they'd all be more interested in getting to know the local guys—intimately.

She made a face. Logan would no doubt be a willing volunteer. She still hadn't figured out his weird behavior in the café earlier. If she had to guess, she'd say that he was probably trying to pique Courtney's interest. He'd probably only come over to make sure that they knew that he'd be at the Boathouse tonight, too. Though that didn't really make sense. Logan wasn't the kind to play games like that. He was more likely to walk up to a girl he was interested in and tell her that he'd be there and that he'd be available to take her home afterward, too. There was no reason for him to let them know that he was her friend.

It didn't matter what he was up to. A little shiver ran down her spine. Whatever it was, it meant that he'd put an arm around her and kissed her forehead. She shouldn't be so pleased about that, but she was. She'd had a crush on him since the first day she met him. He was a safe guy to have a crush on. He was a player, in no uncertain terms. He liked hot chicks—and she could hardly be described as one of those. She could enjoy looking at him without ever worrying that he might return the interest.

Her phone rang, interrupting her thoughts about just how gorgeous he was. She hit the button to answer.

"Hey, Maria. What's up?"

"Hey, Roxy. I'm just leaving work now. I wanted to make sure you're coming tonight."

"I am. I'm looking forward to seeing everyone; it's been a while since I've been out to see the band."

"I know. I just wanted to make sure that you're still coming."

"Why wouldn't I?"

"I heard that some of your old friends are in town for a bachelorette party and that you didn't even know they were coming. Are you okay with that?"

Roxy blew out a sigh. "I'm okay with not knowing they were coming and okay with not being invited. I'm less okay with wondering how on earth you know about it already."

Maria laughed. "You know what this place is like. Gossip travels fast. Zack ran into Aaron at the grocery store, and he told him."

"Wow. I didn't think guys gossiped like that."

"Sure, they do. They're as bad as we are, if not worse. Are you okay with it all?"

"Yeah. I was just thinking that I probably won't see much of the girls. They're more likely to be on the prowl than want to hang out with me."

"Oh. I see. Well, you don't need them, anyway. You've got us now."

Roxy's eyes pricked with tears. "I do, and I love you guys."

"Aww. I love you, too."

"I mean it, Maria. You don't know what it was like when they were my friends. They're … mean, is probably the best word. I always felt second best, second class around them. They were all so much perkier, and prettier and richer—and they didn't mind reminding me about that any chance they got."

"They sound horrible. And no way are they prettier than you. You're beautiful."

Roxy laughed. "You're too sweet. I'm okay. But they do all the clothes and nails and makeup and hair and all that stuff that I never really cared about. I always felt inferior, you know?"

"I hate that! You should never feel that way. I'll tell you what, why don't you come over and get ready with me at our place. I'll do your hair and makeup—I'll lend you something to wear, too, if you want. You show them, and more importantly, show yourself. You'd beat them at their game if you chose to play it. You just have different priorities; you care about more important things."

Roxy thought about it for a moment and smiled. "Would you mind? That'd be kind of awesome. I know it's silly, but I would like them to see me all dolled up and not just the frumpy clueless me they remember."

"Of course. Just come over whenever you want. We'll get ready together."

"Won't Zack mind?"

"No! He was only saying the other day that we hadn't seen much of you lately. He won't hang out for the hair and makeup part, but he'll pick us out a great bottle of wine to enjoy while we're doing it."

"Okay, thanks, Maria. I'll text you before I come to make sure it's okay."

Maria laughed. "It is okay, just come whenever you want. I'll be home in twenty minutes."

Chapter Two

Logan looked up at the sound of a knock on his office door. "Hey, Nate, what's up?"

"Nothing's up with me," said Nate. "I thought everyone had left. I'm surprised to see you still here at this time on a Friday. Is everything okay?"

"Yeah. Everything's fine. I was just working through the list of issues brought up at today's meeting."

Nate smiled. "I love that you call it a meeting, and the guys just think that you treat them to lunch."

Logan grinned back at him. "It comes from having worked my way up through the ranks. I know how much the guys hate having to stop work to attend meetings. Meetings are nonproductive. Lunch is a good chance to hang out with all the guys, and when the guys hang out, they tend to bitch about what's not working."

Nate nodded. "Anything I need to know about?"

"No. It's all good. Everything's on track. We had a couple of issues with delays on supplies. But I spent this afternoon working out the kinks."

"I'm glad to hear it. I don't want to fall behind on this one."

"Nor do I."

"Well, if you're all sorted, are you going to get out of here?"

Logan looked up at the clock on the wall. "Damn! I didn't realize it was that time already."

Nate gave him a knowing smile. "Let me guess; you have a hot date waiting for you?"

Logan shrugged. "I'm heading over to the Boathouse to meet up with everyone."

"Good. I'll see you there then. Lily and I are meeting up with the gang tonight, too. But you didn't answer the question. I can't believe that there isn't a hot chick involved."

Logan smirked. "There isn't always a hot chick."

Nate laughed. "Maybe not always, but at least ninety-nine percent of the time. Josh mentioned that there were some girls in the café at lunchtime. It sounded like he was interested. I can't believe he spotted them, and you didn't."

Logan pursed his lips. He wished those girls hadn't shown up at all. He was still angry about the way they'd talked about Roxy.

Nate raised an eyebrow at him. "Don't tell me you're losing your touch? Did Josh really spot some girls that you didn't?"

Logan laughed. "You're not even seriously asking me that, are you?"

"I wouldn't be. Normally," said Nate. "But the look on your face says something's off."

"Honestly, I had my eye on one of them until I realized that they're old friends of Roxy's. It seems that they're out here for a bachelorette party. But it's just coincidence that they chose Summer Lake for it. They hadn't invited her; they didn't know she lives here."

Nate gave him a puzzled look. "And?"

"And I overheard the way they were talking about her … let's just say they didn't sound like they'd be very good friends to have."

"A lot of us had lives we left behind when we moved here. It sounds like that might be the case for Roxy. She doesn't strike me as someone to be upset by a bunch of mean girls."

Logan laughed. "It's funny you should call them that. That's exactly how they struck me. And no, I don't think Roxy was fazed by it at all. It just rubbed me wrong. They were talking as though they were so superior to her. And Roxy's awesome."

Nate gave him a knowing look. "I've wondered sometimes if you had a thing for her."

"No. It's not that. She's a friend. She's a good girl. I don't like anyone messing with my friends."

Nate nodded. "None of us do. I'm sure Roxy will be fine. And if those girls do give her any kind of a hard time, everyone here will rally around to support her."

Logan nodded. He hated the thought of them giving her a hard time. But it wasn't even that that was bothering him. For some reason, it had irritated him to no end that they saw themselves as so superior to Roxy, when in his eyes, not one of them could hold a candle to her.

Roxy pulled up in front of the big wrought iron gates that stood at the entrance to Maria and Zack's place. She put her window down and reached out to press the buzzer.

"Hey, Roxy. Come on through." Zack's voice sounded tinny through the little speaker.

"Thanks. I'll see you in a minute." Roxy watched as the gates magically slid open and then pulled her car through. She looked around as she drove toward the house. This place was fabulous. Trees lined the driveway, and between them, she could glimpse views of the lake. She was so happy for her friends that they'd managed to overcome Zack's troubles and now got to live happily together in such a wonderful place.

She pulled up in front of the house and smiled when the door opened. Maria always liked to come out to greet her friends when they arrived. This time, though, it wasn't Maria who greeted her with a smile. It was Zack.

"Hey, come on in. Maria just got out of the shower. So, I'm the official greeting party. I picked us out a big, bold Cab since I know you like those."

"Thanks, Zack. You're the best. Are you sure that you don't have a brother just like you?"

Zack laughed. "There was talk at one point that I might have a half-brother somewhere, but I don't think that would be a road you'd want to go down. Anyway, I'm sure you could find yourself a great guy much closer to home."

Roxy laughed. "You'd think so, wouldn't you? Everyone else seems to manage it around here. But not me." She shrugged and rolled her eyes at that. "Anyway, let's not stand here on the steps lamenting my lack of a love life. Not when you have a perfectly good bottle of wine going to waste in there."

She followed Zack through to the kitchen. While he poured her a glass of wine, she took a seat at the huge island and looked out at the beautiful view of the lake. "This is such a lovely house. I'm so happy for you two."

"Thanks. I spent so many years on the move, I never dared think I'd end up settling down in a place like this." He turned his head to look toward the stairs at the sound of Maria coming down. "And I sure as hell didn't think I'd ever be so lucky as to find someone like Maria."

Maria gave him a puzzled look as she came toward them and gave Roxy a hug. "What's he saying about me? Is he telling you what pain in the butt I am?"

"No way," said Roxy with a laugh. "He's telling me what a lucky guy he is. And I happen to agree with him."

"Well, I disagree," said Maria with a smile. She went and planted a kiss on Zack's cheek. "I say I'm the lucky one."

Roxy laughed. "Give it up, would you? I'm very happy for you both, but remember who you're talking to here. I'm the one who hasn't even had a date in forever. I might be happy for you, but I won't deny that I get a teensy bit jealous every now and then."

"Aww." Zack came to her and wrapped his arm around her shoulders. "It's only a matter of timing. Your guy is out there. He just hasn't shown up yet."

"Well, I wish he'd hurry up about it," said Roxy with a laugh.

"Maybe he's shown up already," said Maria. "But you just haven't realized it yet."

Roxy shook her head. "I don't think any of the guys we know are my Mr. Right. You're not seriously saying that you do, are you?"

Maria shrugged. "Maybe. You never know. Zack and I knew each other for a couple of years before we ever got together. So did Angel and Luke."

"Yeah, but we all knew from the beginning that you were supposed to be together. It was obvious that you two liked each other, and Angel and Luke, too. I don't have anyone like that. I mean, come on, in our group of friends, who is there? There's Austin. He's with Nadia, though why none of us knows. Then there's Colt. He's a sweetie pie, but he's not my type, and it's fairly evident that I'm not his."

Maria gave her an odd look. "And you're forgetting the obvious."

"The obvious?"

"Yeah, I don't see anyone obvious," said Zack. "Who do you mean?"

"Are you both playing dumb?" asked Maria. "What about Logan?"

Roxy laughed out loud at that. "What about Logan? Okay, so it's no secret that I think he's good-looking. But come on, Logan isn't anybody's Mr. Right. Although he is a lot of girls' Mr. Right Now."

Zack nodded. "Sorry, but I have to agree with Roxy on that one. Logan's a good guy, a good friend. But I see him as being one of those guys who'll never settle down."

Maria shook her head. "Well, I think you're both wrong. I think he's enjoying sewing his wild oats, but that won't last forever. It's just a phase, and when he's had enough of it, I think we'll get to see a different side of him. I mean, he's a stand-up guy. He's solid and reliable in every other aspect. I think he'd be perfect for you, Rox."

Roxy shook her head adamantly. "And I think you're nuts. If I could transfer his looks onto someone solid and reliable, then yes, I'd be interested. But you're just getting carried away. That's not who he is. Don't get me wrong, I do think he's good guy, but I don't think he'll ever be boyfriend material. He enjoys what he does too much—and he's too good at it to give it up."

"What do you mean?" asked Maria.

Zack laughed. "I think she means he's too good at sleeping around and sorry, but I have to agree with her."

Roxy gave him a rueful smile. Zack was right. He was a realist. Maria tended to look on the bright side of everything—and sometimes she ignored reality in order to do so.

Maria shrugged. "Maybe you're both right, but I have a sneaky feeling that Logan might prove you wrong one of these days. He has a good heart. But tonight isn't about him; it's about getting you all done up so you can show those girls you used to know just how beautiful you are."

Roxy made a face at Zack. "She's going to have her work cut out for her."

"Give yourself some credit, Rox. I'm going to leave you both to it, but I know full well that you'll both look stunning when you're done."

"Aww." Roxy punched his arm. "You're a good 'un. Thanks. I'm sorry I'm crashing your evening, but I appreciate you letting me."

"You're not crashing anything. I'm going to call my dad, which is exactly what I planned to do while Maria was getting ready."

Maria picked up the glass of wine he'd poured for her. "Give him my love, won't you? And ask when he's coming to visit again."

Roxy followed her upstairs and looked around in wonder as Maria led her into her dressing room. "I *love* this place!"

Maria laughed. "I do, too. I still can't quite believe it's real. That I live here. That Zack and I are together."

"That you're getting married. It's awesome."

Maria nodded happily. "It is. And sorry I went on about Logan before. It's just that I'm so happy. I want the same for you."

"Hey. Don't be sorry. I want it, too. But, unfortunately, even when I do find my person, it won't be Logan."

"If you say so. But don't rule out the idea completely. I know he's not boyfriend material right now, but I seriously believe that he'll be ready to straighten up his act at some point, and when he does, he'll be a real catch."

Roxy gave her a sad smile. "I won't rule the idea out—in fact, since it's you, I'll admit that I daydream about it sometimes. But I'm more of a realist than you are. Just because he's gorgeous to look at, it's not enough. He's a player. We all know that. And even when a guy grows out of that kind of thing, you have to ask yourself what it is about his personality that makes him think that it's okay to live that way. It brings up the question of values, and it's evident that his and mine don't match."

Maria blew out a sigh. "I'm not going to argue with you. I still think you could be wrong. But it's time to change the subject." She grinned and opened the door to her closet. "It's time to find you something to wear."

Roxy grinned back at her. Maria wore such lovely clothes. She was one of those girls who was always so well put together. In fact, when Roxy had first met her, she'd been a little intimidated. Maria had struck her as being like the girls she'd gone to college with. But, although Maria was like them in that she took great care of the way she looked and cared about her hair and makeup, she couldn't be more different from them in all the ways that mattered. She was kind and caring. She looked out for her friends, and she certainly didn't judge people by where they came from or what they had.

Logan ran down the stairs to get the door and smiled when he opened it and saw Austin standing there.

"Hey, come on in. What are you doing here? I thought you were going with Nadia tonight."

Austin rolled his eyes and stepped inside. "She's pissed at me again. I don't even know what I did wrong this time. She says she doesn't want to go anywhere with me tonight. And I'm tired of it. She does this way too often, and she expects me to go home and sit there feeling sorry for myself. Well, I'm not doing it again. I've been looking forward to seeing everyone and to hearing the band. I'm going anyway."

Logan raised his eyebrows. "And you're prepared to deal with her wrath when she hears that you dared go without her permission?"

"I'm done with getting her permission and dealing with her sulking. I told her. I'm done."

"Wow. Are you serious?"

"Never been more serious in my life. I should've listened to you guys a long time ago. I can't take it anymore."

Logan grasped his shoulder. "For what it's worth, I think you're doing the right thing. I know I give you a hard time about her. It's no secret that I can't stand her, but what I dislike most about her is that she makes you miserable. You only get one life, bud. You can't waste it spending time with someone who makes you unhappy."

Austin gave him a rueful smile. "I know. I've known it for a long time. I just didn't have the balls to do anything about it. I felt guilty wanting to do stuff for myself; she *made* me feel guilty—like anything I did to make myself happy made her miserable."

"Some people are like that. They think you exist for their convenience. I'm glad you've escaped her clutches before it's too late. For a while there, I thought you were going to end up marrying her and wasting your whole life."

Austin shuddered. "For a while there so did I, but something just snapped in my head tonight. It's not my responsibility to make her happy. It's hers. And if she can't manage to do that, it's not my fault—and not something I want to stick around to witness."

Logan went to the fridge and took out two bottles of beer. "I'd say that you coming to your senses calls for a celebration. Here you go."

Austin took one from him with a smile. "Thanks."

Logan raised his beer with a grin. "Here's to your freedom."

Austin laughed. "Yep, long may it last. I'm thinking I should follow your example in the future and stay single. Caring about people just makes you miserable."

Logan frowned. "No. That's not the way I see it. Caring about people is what makes life worth living."

Austin laughed. "You're not telling me that you care about all the women you sleep with?"

"No. I mean that I care about the people in my life. You don't sleep with people that you care about."

"What?"

Logan grinned. "It's true. I divide people into friends and fucks. And ne'er the twain shall meet. Sex is for fun—but you don't confuse it with friendship. Friends are worth so much more than a quick roll in the sack."

Austin stared at him for a long moment. "Is that seriously how you see it?"

Logan nodded solemnly.

"But sex is supposed to be something that you share with someone who you care about."

"Not in my world. The way I see it, if you care about them, you stay the hell away from anything physical. And if you're getting into something physical, then the last thing you want to do is start caring about them. It complicates everything, and I like life simple."

Austin was staring at him as if he were crazy.

Logan shrugged. "You don't have to agree with me. It's just my way. But tell me this; which one of us is happy and enjoying life and which one's been miserable for the last couple of years?"

Austin blew out a sigh.

"I rest my case. Now come on, down your beer and let's get going. I hope you walked over here. Neither of us is driving tonight."

Chapter Three

When they arrived at the Boathouse, Logan wasn't surprised to see Roxy's friends sitting at the table right by the stage. Girls like that would want to be upfront and visible to everyone in the place—and close to the band, too.

He smirked to himself when he saw one of them making eyes at Chase, the lead singer. She wouldn't have any luck there. Chase was as happily married as any guy Logan had ever known and ... yep, there she came. His wife Kenzie had come out from behind the bar, and in their usual style, Chase pulled her in for a kiss that told anyone with eyes in their head who he'd be going home with later—and left no doubt about what they'd be doing when they got there. When he let her go, Kenzie went over to the girls table and smiled around at them.

Logan guessed that she was asking if they needed more drinks, but what she was really doing was telling them that Chase was off-limits. He chuckled to himself. The mating rituals of the female of the species amused him greatly. Whether they were trying to attract a mate or keep a mate, their actions spoke loudly to anyone who paid attention—and he paid attention. Usually, it was to select his partner in fun for the next few hours. Tonight, he was curious about Roxy's friends. He had the feeling—and from what he'd just seen, he was right—that they were the kind who were out looking to get laid. Normally, he'd have his sights set on one of them, and possibly a second as a backup option. Not tonight, though. Tonight, he was watching them as a potential threat to Roxy. That was a crazy thought. They weren't a threat, and even if they were, it wasn't his place to protect her, but somehow, it felt like it was.

Austin nudged him with his elbow. "You go do your thing if you like. I don't need babysitting and Colt's over there with Angel and Luke. The others will no doubt be along soon. I wouldn't want to cramp your style, but I'm not up to being your wingman yet. Maybe next weekend."

Logan shook his head with a smile. "Nah. I'm not interested in those girls. They're Roxy's old friends."

Austin laughed. "What and she'd kill you if you made a move on them?"

"No. I heard them talking about her at the café at lunchtime today, and they're shitty people. Roxy doesn't know it, though. I just hope they stay away from her, and if I have to, I'll make sure they do."

Austin raised an eyebrow at him. "Are you finally ready to come out and admit that you like her?"

"I've always liked her. She's my friend."

Austin pursed his lips. "You know what I mean."

Logan stared at him for a long moment. "Sure, I think she's gorgeous, but like I said, she's my friend."

"So, you're sticking with your friends and fucks theory, and there's no way a woman can be both?"

A shiver ran down Logan's back. The words *Roxy* and *fuck* shouldn't be allowed in the same sentence as far as he was concerned. That was dangerous territory. Even if he occasionally saw her face when there was another woman underneath him, that was just fantasy. Not reality. It couldn't ever be reality. He cared about her too much for that.

Austin waved a hand in front of his face. "Hello? Did I lose you?"

Logan grinned. "No. Sorry. My circuits just got jammed thinking about Roxy and me like that. We're not like that. We never could be."

"Sure, you could. If you were ready to give up your ways."

Logan's heart skipped a couple of beats. That was a possibility he hadn't considered before. He stared at Austin. "You think?"

Austin laughed. "I do. You should consider it. It's obvious you like her, and from the way she's so prickly with you, I'd guess that she likes you, too."

"Hey, guys." Colt appeared at Logan's side. "What's up?"

"Hey, Colt. How's it going?"

"I'm good. I was starting to wonder if you were coming over or not. Are you? Or are you planning to introduce yourself to those lovely ladies who are all watching you like hawks?" He grinned at Austin. "I know you're not going over there. Where's Nadia?"

Austin blew out a sigh. "Not coming."

As Logan listened to Austin explain to Colt that he'd finally broken up with Nadia, the bouncy brunette caught his eye and gave him a wave. He nodded but didn't smile. Unfortunately for him, that wasn't enough to put her off. She got to her feet and made her way over to them.

"I'll catch you later, guys." Logan left the others to meet her before she reached them.

"Hi. I was hoping you'd be here. I'm Courtney."

Logan let his gaze travel over her slowly. Any other time, he'd be appreciating her long, lean body and those breasts, which he now decided were definitely not God-given. "Hi, Courtney." When he finally met her gaze, the look she gave him told him everything he needed to know. If she weren't

Roxy's so-called friend, he probably would have asked her if she wanted to get out of here right now—and he was ninety-nine percent certain that she would have said yes.

"You're a friend of Roxy's, aren't you?"

He nodded. "I am."

She surprised him by taking hold of his hand. "You should come and meet the rest of the girls. We went to college with her."

He let her lead him over to the table where all the girls were watching him.

"Are you with her?" asked Courtney just before they reached the others.

He shook his head but didn't answer, wondering what she was after. He had this nasty feeling that she was the kind of girl who'd make an extra play for him if she thought he was someone's boyfriend.

She chuckled. "I didn't think you could be. I mean …" She ran her hand up his arm. "You're in a different league."

He wanted to shrug her hand away and tell her what he thought of her. Instead, he followed her gaze when her eyes widened, and she muttered, "Damn!"

He echoed the sentiment at the sight of Roxy, who was now standing talking to Austin and Colt. She looked amazing. She always looked good to him, but she wasn't one of those girls who went out of her way to turn up the heat—usually. Tonight, his temperature soared at the sight of her in a short, V-necked dress paired with cowboy boots. Her hair was different, her face was even prettier than usual. Either he was going nuts, or she'd done something very different with herself tonight. And he liked it—a lot.

She turned as if she felt his gaze on her and smiled when she saw him. It made his heart race. He was too used to her smile disappearing when she spotted him, but this felt as though she was pleased to see him. He wasn't used to that.

Her smile did its usual disappearing act when she spotted Courtney standing beside him. Damn. He didn't want her to think he was interested. He wasn't. He was only talking to her to try to figure out how mean these girls were and what Roxy needed to know, so they didn't hurt her.

Courtney smiled and waved Roxy over then turned back to Logan. "You made me wonder this afternoon in the café, I thought you were with her. But even then, I had a feeling you'd be coming with me tonight. You're the kind of guy who likes to play, right?"

Logan pursed his lips. "I am, but I won't be going anywhere with you. I'm not with Roxy because she's too smart to have me. But that doesn't mean I wouldn't like to be. She's worth a hundred of you. We both know that there's a one hundred percent chance of me getting with you tonight, and I know there's less than a one percent chance with Roxy, but I'm more interested in that tiny chance than I am in you."

Courtney glared at him, and he froze when he heard Roxy clear her throat beside him. He turned to look at her. To say she was shocked by his words was an understatement.

Courtney glared at him, too, then turned on her heel and went back to the table.

Logan's heart raced as the silence between him and Roxy lengthened. She held his gaze and eventually cocked her head to one side and asked, "What are you playing at?"

He shrugged. He didn't know how to tell her that for once in his life, he wasn't playing anyone. He'd told Courtney the truth as he saw it; he just hadn't expected Roxy to overhear it.

She shook her head. "I know you'll say anything to get a girl into bed, but I don't see how that tactic would work. Maybe showing a little interest in another girl might pique her interest, but saying something like you just did? That's more likely to piss her off."

He closed his eyes for a moment. Jesus. She'd just heard him admit how much he liked her and she thought it was some kind of game he was playing to make another girl jealous? What kind of monster did she think he was?

"Can I talk to you for a minute?" He took hold of her arm and led her away from the table where Courtney and the others were all watching them.

She scowled but went with him and didn't pull her arm away. He didn't stop until they were out on the deck. It was cold out here, and the big heaters didn't reach the railing over the water where he finally stopped, but there was a heat rushing through him at being this close to her.

"What on earth is going on with you?"

He gave her a sheepish grin. "I'm making an idiot of myself."

She didn't try to hide her smile. "I knew that much. What I can't figure out is why."

"Those girls ..." He hesitated. He wanted to tell her what he thought of them, but he wasn't sure if she'd get defensive about them, or if he'd hurt her feelings when she found out what they really thought of her.

She made a face and shook her head. "I normally keep my mouth shut about the women you choose to ... spend time with. It's none of my business, but, as a friend, I wish you'd find someone else."

"I'm not even thinking about it, Rox. I know you think they're your friends."

She raised an eyebrow at him. "Why did you put it like that? I *think* they're my friends?"

He swallowed. There was no backing out now. "Listen. I'm sorry. I don't want to hurt your feelings, but they're ... not nice. They're not such good friends as you think they are."

To his surprise, she laughed.

"No, seriously, Rox. I'm not making shit up. I'm not interested in them. I'm interested in you not getting hurt. They …" He didn't want to tell her what he'd heard them saying about her at lunchtime. "They're mean."

She laughed again. "I know that much."

"You do?"

She nodded. "You chose the perfect word. They're like a bunch of mean girls. They were my friends in college—at least, I thought they were, but even then, I felt like a second-class citizen around them."

"That's crazy. They've got nothing next to you."

She made a face. "I appreciate you looking out for me, I really do. I think it's sweet of you. But you don't need to lay it on so thick. They're the pretty girls, the popular girls. I'm just me. If you want to go after one of them, I don't mind. As long as you know what they're like. But then, I don't suppose their personality matters much to you."

He pursed his lips and gave her a hard stare. "I'm not interested. I told you. I'm only concerned about you."

"Hey. Are you okay?"

They both turned at the sound of Maria's voice. Logan liked her. He was usually glad to see her, but he wished she'd give them a minute.

"What's going on, guys?"

~ ~ ~

"Can you believe that Logan had already run into the girls, and he's figured out what they're like. He was trying to warn me about them—or protect my feelings, or …" Roxy wasn't exactly sure what he'd been trying to do. She'd be forever grateful to him for what he'd said about her being worth a hundred of Courtney, but she didn't get why he'd said it. He did tend to be protective of all his friends, so she'd guess that was it.

To her surprise, Maria grinned at Logan. "Well, aren't you the sweetest? Roxy told me about them this afternoon. She doesn't need that kind of negativity in her life."

Roxy shrugged. "They're not in my life anymore, I'm happy to say. It was just a rude reminder today. I used to feel so much less than them back then. They were so pretty; they were the popular ones; they dated the hot guys. I was just the tag-along-friend."

"Well, you're not anymore. You're the one who has it all now. Look at you. Not one of them is as pretty as you are. Are they, Logan?"

"Don't put him on the spot like that, it's not fair," said Roxy. She didn't want him to have to say something that he didn't mean.

He surprised the hell out of her as he let his gaze run over her, obviously appreciating what he saw. He nodded as he met her eye. "Can't even come close," he breathed.

A shudder ran down her spine as she looked back into his eyes. If she didn't already know what he was like—the power he had over women and his ability to make them drop their panties, she'd believe that he was as interested in her as he looked—and she'd be willing to explore that interest with him.

Instead, she waved a hand at him. "Thanks, but you've both done all you need to build my fragile ego back up. You don't need to lay it on too thick."

His head jerked back, and a shadow of something she didn't understand crossed his face. "I'm just saying it like it is, Rox. You're gorgeous."

He said stuff like that all the time—to her and to Maria and Angel, and Amber and Jade and all of their friends. It was just his way. He might look serious, he might sound different than he usually did, but it was just …

She didn't have a chance to finish the thought as Maria slapped her arm. "You know what you should do? You should act as though you two are together. Wouldn't it feel good to be with the guy that they all want but can't have?"

Roxy blurted out a laugh. She wasn't about to admit just how good that would feel. But she couldn't do it—even aside from the fact that Logan wouldn't want it. If he pretended to be with her, he wouldn't be able to make a move on whoever he *was* going to be with later. There was bound to be someone. He rarely left the Boathouse without a girl on his arm on a Friday night.

She turned to look at him, expecting to see a horrified look on his face and hear him make excuses about why that would be a bad idea. Instead, he was grinning.

"I think that's an awesome idea, Rox. What do you say? Want to be my girlfriend for the night?"

She laughed. "Why would you even want to?"

He hesitated for a moment and then shrugged. "Because they made you feel bad. If I can help you feel good, then I'm all in."

She had to press her lips together. She knew he'd be able to make her feel good. She fantasized about it often enough. But she had to pull herself together. That wasn't what he was talking about. She smiled at him. He was talking about being a real friend, and that meant a lot. "Are you sure? I know there are other things you'd rather be doing with your Friday night—I don't want to screw that up for you."

He smiled. "It'll be my pleasure. Helping you out is much more important."

"That's right," said Maria, who Roxy had almost forgotten was still there. "He can hang out with a random chick any weekend he chooses. This is his one and only chance to do this." She gave Logan a meaningful look. Roxy just wished she understood what the meaning was.

Chapter Four

"Where did Roxy disappear to?" asked Lucy. "I thought she was coming over. And where's that guy gone—the one from the café earlier? I thought you'd snagged him, Courtney."

Courtney made a face. "So did I, but apparently he has a thing for Roxy. They went outside together."

"Wow." Lucy smiled. "Who'd have thought she could land a guy like that? Good for her."

Jana laughed. "Don't look like that, Courtney. I'm sure he'd choose you if he'd met you both at the same time."

Courtney shrugged. Normally, she'd be sure of that, too. But what Logan had said? That Roxy was worth a hundred of her? That had stung. It wasn't true, of course. Roxy was a nobody. But then Logan was just a small-town guy who didn't know what he was talking about. Still, she hadn't liked hearing it. She was used to guys making a play for her, not snubbing her in favor of a dowdy one-time friend.

"Never mind," said Lucy. "There are lots of hot guys here. I'm sure you'll find yourself another one before the night is out."

Courtney scanned the bar. It was true. There seemed to be an unusually high percentage of hot guys in this place. Many of them were with partners, but there were still plenty who seemed to be single. Her gaze came to rest on the guy who Logan had come with. He wasn't quite as good-looking as Logan. He was fairer and seemed less outgoing, but he was built and had a strong jawline and gorgeous eyes. She watched as he chatted with a group of friends. It looked like he was explaining something to them—something that made them look happy even though he didn't seem too happy about it.

"What's up?" asked Jana. "Have you selected your next victim?"

She smiled as she saw Logan and Roxy join the group. "Yes, I think I have. I'm going to say hi to Roxy. I'll be back."

Roxy couldn't help but smile when she heard Austin's news that he and Nadia had broken up. She felt bad because, although he was saying he was relieved, he looked a bit down. She gave him a hug and stepped back with a smile. "You'll be okay. It might take you a while; you two have been together for a long time, but it's for the best. You haven't been happy with her for as long as I can remember."

He nodded and gave her a grateful smile. "Thanks, Roxy. I know you're right. My first reaction was just a big sigh of relief, but now it's hitting me."

Maria smiled at him. "It will do, but you'll get past it. You'll miss the routine that you'd fallen into with her, but it wasn't a healthy routine."

"I know. I'll be okay." He smiled around at them all. "Any chance we can change the subject?"

Logan punched his arm. "Sure, we can, but before we do, tell me—is it because you don't like being the center of attention, or because you've spotted the same people I have and you don't want one of them to hear this?"

Roxy followed Logan's gaze as he jerked his chin to where Amber and Jade were making their way through the bar to join them. She smiled to herself. She had a feeling Austin might not take too long at all to get over his breakup with Nadia. They'd all suspected that he had a thing for Amber ever since the sisters had arrived in town. Now that he was single, there was nothing stopping him from asking her out—and Roxy had a feeling that she'd say yes.

Her smile faded when she spotted Courtney a few steps behind Amber and Jade. It looked like she was coming this way, too.

Logan must have spotted her at the same moment; he edged closer to Roxy and slung his arm around her shoulders, sending a thrill racing through her. She knew he was only doing it for appearance's sake, but she leaned closer into him—there was no reason not to make the most of it.

Amber and Jade reached the group a few steps ahead of Courtney, and Jade raised an eyebrow at Logan.

"Is there something we don't know about going on here, or do you have a death wish?"

Roxy chuckled. It was a well-known part of the dynamics of their group that Logan flirted with all the girls and, mostly, they humored him. She was the only one who consistently put him in his place.

Logan drew her closer into his side. "I'm on a suicide mission," he told Jade with a grin. "She's blocked my advances for so long that I've grown desperate. I'm going all in on a last-ditch attempt to make her mine. Do or die."

Even as Roxy laughed, she wished it was true.

"Hi, Roxy. I thought you were coming over to see us."

All heads turned to Courtney as she joined the group of them standing there, and Roxy didn't miss the fact that both

Austin and Colt's eyes lingered on her longer than was necessary.

"I was on my way, but this guy waylaid me." She was grateful that Logan tightened his arm around her. It felt so good—in a purely physical way, and even more than that, it felt good to have his emotional support. He didn't know the whole story, but he had some idea of how Courtney had made her feel, and he was letting her know he was there for her—he had her back, and that meant a lot.

"Yeah, sorry," said Logan. "I don't know when I can let you have her back."

Roxy shuddered at the way Courtney smiled at him. "No worries. I'm sure it won't be too long before you're done with her."

Ouch. Roxy was absolutely certain that she meant that to sound as harsh as it did. It appeared some of the others picked up on it, too.

Maria turned to Courtney with a smile that Roxy knew held trouble. "You're one of the friends from college, aren't you?"

"I am. I'm Courtney."

To Roxy's dismay, Colt stepped forward to shake hands with her. "Any friend of Roxy's is welcome here," he said with a smile.

Courtney shook with him and turned on the charm. "That's so sweet of you. You should come over and meet her other friends, too. And you," she added, nodding at Austin.

Roxy watched as she led the only two obviously single guys away toward the table where the rest of the girls were sitting.

"I guess that's the last we'll see of them tonight," said Amber.

"Don't worry," said Logan. "They'll be back."

"I wasn't worried," Amber replied a little too quickly, making Roxy suspect that all her protests about not being interested in

Austin weren't true. Amber would never have admitted that she liked him while he had a girlfriend … but now he didn't.

"Never mind them. What's going on with you two?" Luke looked at Roxy and Logan, whose arm still rested around her shoulders.

"Nothing," said Roxy with a smile. "He's just being a gentleman and helping me out."

Luke grinned. "A gentleman?"

"It looks to me more like he wants to help himself out," said Jade.

Logan laughed. "I'm not always a predator. I'm looking out for my friend here. Those girls are bitchy."

Maria nodded at his side. "You know, normally I'd agree with you, Jade. Our Logan is usually out for what he can get with the ladies, but this time he's being a hero."

Roxy looked up at him. "Did you hear that? You're a hero."

"How?" asked Jade. "I don't get it."

"At college, I was the frumpy one," Roxy explained. "They were the pretty, popular girls. I didn't want them to see me like that now. So, Maria dressed me up, and Logan is pretending that he's interested in me." She gave a self-conscious laugh. "I know it probably sounds stupid—because I admit, it is stupid. I just didn't want to feel the way I used to feel around them. I wanted them to think that I'm better than that."

"It's not stupid," said Jade. "I get it. I think at some point, we've all wished that we could show people from our past how great we're doing now." She raised an eyebrow at Logan. "I'd just watch this one. Don't let him keep up the act when there's no one around to see it."

Roxy laughed. "Don't worry. He's hardly likely to do that; it's just for show." She was surprised at the looks some of the others gave her. Luke, in particular, looked skeptical.

~ ~ ~

It was a great evening. He often missed out on hanging out with everyone on nights like this because he was busy chatting to girls. Tonight was reminding him just what a great group this was. As the night drew on, he resolved to spend more time with them and less time chasing women. He cocked an eyebrow at Roxy as they watched Maria and Zack follow Angel and Luke out on to the dance floor. It was getting late, and the band usually finished their set with a few slow ballads to let the couples dance.

Roxy gave him a puzzled look. "Something up?"

He had to hide a smile. "May I have the honor of this dance?"

She looked at the couples already swaying to the music then back at him. "Are you serious?"

He nodded solemnly. "Never been more so." He got to his feet and held his hand out to her, hoping that would be enough to persuade her that he was, indeed, serious.

She got up and let him lead her onto the floor. She looked up at him as he slid an arm around her waist and drew her toward him. She only hesitated a moment before she looped her arms up around his neck.

He had to bite the inside of his cheek when he dared tighten his arms around her and hold her close to his chest. She felt so damned good! He closed his eyes briefly, but that didn't help—he saw images of them in bed together when he did that. When he opened them again, she was looking up into them.

"Are you okay?"

He nodded and made himself grin at her. He needed to keep up his usual banter. He couldn't afford to get caught up in the moment. He picked up his pace and whirled her around to the music, making her laugh, and to his relief, putting a couple of inches of air between their bodies, giving himself a chance to calm back down.

When the song came to an end, she made to leave, but he held her closer as the band started to sing an old love song. It was one his grandma used to play when he was a kid. "Stay?"

She searched his face for a moment before she nodded and rested her head against his shoulder.

Logan closed his eyes and let himself get lost in the feel of her soft body pressed against his, the fresh scent of her hair in his nostrils, and the warm, happy nostalgia that the song filled his heart with. He held her close as they swayed together. He was no stranger to these slow dances at the end of an evening. Usually, they were the first chance to get closer to the body he was holding. He opened his eyes, and his heart started to race when the thought occurred to him that this was his first chance to get closer to the woman he was holding.

She sensed the change in him and looked up into his eyes. "Are you okay?"

He cupped the back of her head with his hand. He didn't want to let her see what he was thinking, and he was afraid it must be written all over his face. For a crazy moment, he lowered his lips toward hers, but instead of moving in for a kiss, he cradled her head back against his shoulder. "I'm great, Rox," he murmured. "Just great."

When the music finally ended, she stepped away from him. "Thanks."

"What for?"

She smiled. "I know you always dance these dances, but I only ever get to sit and watch. I know this is only pretend, but it felt good to get to be one of the girls up here for once."

He slid his arm around her shoulders as they walked off the dancefloor. "I always feel bad for the girls up here dancing at the end."

"Bad for them? Why?"

He laughed. "Well, you know most guys think of these slow ballads as the erection section, right? Pretty much every girl up here dancing is letting the world know that she'll be getting laid later."

Roxy sputtered. It looked like half laugh, half indignation. "The erection section? Seriously? That's what you call it?"

He gave her a sheepish grin. "Just don't ever let on that I told you that. It's kind of like bro-code, you know?"

She laughed. "I had no idea. No. And you seriously see it that all the girls dancing to the slowies at the end are going to … you know, later?"

He held his hands out and shrugged. "Look around you."

He followed her gaze as she took in Angel and Luke, Maria and Zack, and several other couples. He hadn't noticed Nate until now, but he was out there with his fiancée, Lily. There were quite a few tourists, some looked like they were couples—others as though they were about to embark on vacation flings.

Roxy looked back at him. "You're right!"

He laughed. "I always am. You should know that by now."

She slapped his arm. "And full of yourself, too."

"Nah, I'm not full of myself tonight."

"Why not?"

He cocked his head to one side. "Because I'm not still out there."

He was trying to let her know that he wished he were, but she took it the wrong way.

Her smile disappeared. "I'm sorry. I totally forgot that I was cramping your style." She looked around quickly. "You're a quick worker. I'll bet there's a bunch of girls here who'd jump up and dance with you right now—and fall in with your theory of what that means."

She continued to scan the room as if seeking him out a partner. He put his hand on her shoulder and waited until she looked back at him. "That's not what I mean, Rox. I meant I wish *we* were still out there."

"Oh." She held his gaze for a long moment before she eventually smiled. "I do, too."

His heart leapt in his chest. "You do?"

"Of course, I do. You must know that."

"I had no idea."

She shrugged. "It doesn't matter, does it? We're friends. I could never go there because I like you too much as a friend. I'd hate to lose that. But that doesn't mean I haven't thought about it."

He could feel the blood pounding in his temples—and in the front of his pants—at the thought that she'd even considered … But she was right. You didn't do that with friends. But, damn, right now, he wanted to.

~ ~ ~

Roxy ran her wrists under the faucet in the bathroom, hoping that it would cool her off. Dancing with Logan like that—and then their conversation afterward—had left her a little over-heated. She turned when the door opened and was relieved to see Maria come in.

"There you are. I wondered where you'd disappeared to."

"I just needed a minute."

"Are you okay?"

"I'm fine. I think I'm going to head home."

"I hope you're going to let Logan take you."

In her attempt to hold back a laugh, Roxy snorted. "I'd love to! In every sense of the term. But I don't think it's a good idea either way."

Maria smiled. "I do. I told you he's a good guy, and I think he's proved it tonight, don't you?"

"Yeah." Roxy smiled, remembering the way she'd felt when he'd pulled her into his side, and when she'd heard him tell Courtney that she was worth so much more than her. "He's been great. He's a much better friend than I gave him credit for."

Maria gave her a stern look. "That's not what I mean, and you know it. He likes you. It's obvious. You should give him a chance—see where it leads."

"That's the trouble, though. I know exactly where it would lead, and so do you. It'd lead straight to bed, mine or his, or the back of his truck on the way there. And I'm sure it'd be amazing. But I'm not like that, Maria. I couldn't just sleep with him and then pretend everything was normal—that nothing had changed. It'd be too weird to just be another of his conquests."

"I don't think you would be. I think it could be more than that."

"No. That's who he is. It's what he does. I'm not going to go fooling myself that he'd give all that up for me." She blew out a sigh. "I'm stupid, and I know it, but I don't believe in just sleeping with people for fun. I need it to be part of something bigger. Logan doesn't work that way. It's only fun to him. It wouldn't be right."

Maria shrugged. "I know that's what his track record has been, but I think you should give him a chance."

Roxy laughed. "I'd love to. But I'm not interested in being just another name on his list, and he wouldn't be interested in the only kind of chance I'd give him."

"You don't think he would be—but you don't know. All I'm saying is don't just assume. Stay open to possibilities."

Roxy dried her hands and nodded. "Okay. But I'm going back out there, and I'm saying goodnight. It's time for me to go home."

"I'll be out in a minute. Don't leave before I get there."

Roxy looked around for the girls as she made her way back to the table where the gang were sitting. Courtney was standing by a pillar talking to a guy—a guy she was relieved to see was neither Austin nor Colt. Lucy and Jana were picking up their purses, looking as though they were ready to leave, and the others were already on their feet. Roxy started to change course to go and say goodnight to them, but she thought better of it. If they wanted to see her, they could come to her. She'd done enough running after them, and she finally understood that she didn't need to.

When she reached the table, Amber and Jade were getting ready to leave. Amber gave her a hug, and Jade grinned at her. "We'll see you soon, and don't forget—watch yourself with him." She jerked her head at Logan.

Logan grinned and came to join them. "Did I hear my name?"

Jade made a face at him. "Yeah. You behave yourself. Roxy's a good girl, and don't you forget it."

Roxy dropped her gaze. Jade could be outspoken, and sometimes it was fun, but this was a little too much.

Logan came and stood beside her and put his arm around her shoulders. "How could I forget it? She's way too good for me."

Jade laughed. "As long as you know that."

She and her sister said goodbye to everyone and left. Roxy looked up at Logan. "Thanks for tonight. I'm going to head off now, too. I'll see you around."

His smile faded. "You'll see me around? Is that it? I thought we were going to show those mean girls? If you leave here alone, it won't work. Let me walk you home?"

Her heart caught in her throat. For a moment, she wished he was asking her for real—that he wanted to walk her home and that maybe they'd kiss, maybe she'd invite him in and … but she came back to her senses. That was the whole point. She couldn't invite him and everything that came after that, because it wouldn't mean anything to him. At least, not anything more than another Friday night filled by another willing body underneath him. The way her tummy flipped when he stroked his fingertips over her shoulder reminded her just how willing her body would be.

"You should go now," said Maria, who had apparently returned from the bathroom and appeared out of nowhere.

"Why?" asked Roxy.

Maria gave her a hard stare. "Just go."

Logan grinned and steered her out of the bar.

"What was that all about?" asked Roxy.

"I don't know, I'm just taking advantage of it." They reached the door, and he held it open for her to go ahead of him.

Once they were outside, she looked up at him. "Why do you even want to walk me home?"

He held her gaze for a long moment, then shrugged. "Because I like you, Rox. I enjoy your company. Isn't that enough?"

She relaxed at that. "Of course, it is. I'm sorry. I think I'm just weirded out by everything. With the girls showing up and you being so nice … so … out of character."

He laughed. "Thanks. So, you think me being nice is out of character?"

"Oh, God, no! I'm sorry. I didn't mean it like that. I meant you not doing your thing, you hanging out with me instead of chasing a woman tonight."

He slung his arm around her shoulders as they walked and looked down into her eyes. "Who says I'm not chasing a woman?"

Chapter Five

Logan had to ask himself what he was playing at. He was walking away from the Boathouse on a Friday with his arm around a beautiful woman—nothing unusual about that. What was unusual was that he knew full well that there was no way he was going to spend the night with her. Worse than that was that he knew she wouldn't sleep with him even if he tried. He didn't know what he was doing, but he did know that something had changed.

When he'd woken up this morning, it was just a regular Friday. He'd known what lay ahead of him—a day of work, an evening of fun, and a night-time in some woman's bed. Now it wasn't a regular Friday anymore. It felt like it was the day that had changed everything. The day that he'd realized that the woman walking beside him was a woman he wanted to spend more time with—he'd always known she was a woman he wanted to sleep with. He sighed and tightened his arm around her shoulders.

"You don't need to go all the way with me, you know."

He couldn't help but chuckle. "But, Rox, there's nothing I want more than to go all the way with you."

She laughed and pushed at his arm. "You know what I mean. You could peel off two blocks before me and get home to bed. I'll be fine."

"No way. You might not want me to take you all the way …" he smirked at her, "but I'm at least going to walk you all the way up to your door, so I know you got home safe."

She made a face. "Okay, thank you."

They walked on in silence for a little while. Logan had so much he wanted to say, but he had no idea where to start, and he had a feeling that no matter what he said, she'd think that he was either joking or worse, trying to get her into bed.

"What was your story with those girls?" he asked eventually. It wasn't safe to say anything about how he was feeling. It'd be better to ask her to talk more about herself. He realized now that he knew so little about her.

"I met them at college. It was a small, liberal arts college. Very exclusive. They were all there on family money—just spending four years going to parties and having fun."

"How did you fall in with them? They don't strike me as your kind of people."

She shrugged. "At that point in my life, I didn't have any kind of people. I was very shy, not social. I'd grown up in a very sheltered life."

"Wow. I would never have guessed that about you."

"Are you making fun of me?"

"No! Hell, no. I mean it. You're so outgoing and down-to-earth. You're friends with everyone."

"I've come out of my shell a lot in the last few years, but I still don't have many friends. I have Maria and Angel, and that's about it, really. I know other people, and everyone here is so friendly, but …"

"And me. You have me and Colt and Austin and Luke and Zack."

She smiled. "I know, but it's not like we're close, really, is it. We hang out as part of the same group, but that's about it. I know I could turn to any of you if ever I needed anything, but you know what I mean. We're not real friends."

He was surprised how much that hurt. It shouldn't, really. He hadn't acted like a true friend toward her, until tonight. She was right. "I think of you as my friend."

"Thanks. I'm not saying I don't think of you as one, but you know what I mean. My point was that I glommed onto Lucy and Jana in college, and they let me hang around, but I always felt kind of inferior. If I'm honest, I think they only kept me around because Courtney had a thing for my brother, and Lucy felt sorry for me. To make things worse, they were all from money, and I was there on a full ride scholarship."

Logan shook his head. "It's so strange to hear what it was like for you. I've always seen you as this super-confident, super-together hot chick. You're a bit intimidating if I'm honest. I can't imagine you feeling second best to those girls. They're ten-a-penny, and you're one-in-a-million."

"Aww." She leaned her head on his shoulder and looked up into his eyes, making his heart beat faster. He came back down to earth at her next words. "I can see how you sweet-talk all those women into bed; you know all the right lines."

"It's not a line, Rox. I mean it."

"Yeah, right. Remember who you're talking to. It's only me. You don't need to bullshit me."

He stopped walking and caught hold of her arm, pulling her back to him. "I'm not. I'd never bullshit you."

Her eyes widened when he put his hands on her shoulders and looked down into her eyes. "You're gorgeous, and you're smart and real, and even though, apparently, you don't think of me as a real friend, I think of you as one. I'm not feeding you lines to make you feel better.

I'm being honest about the way I see you compared to the way I see those girls—and the way I see most women. You're so much more, so much better."

He hoped she'd believe him, but instead, she laughed. "Ha. I'm so much better than them, but they're the ones you want to sleep with?"

He sucked in a deep breath. "That's just sex."

She shook her head. "I know. I'm sorry. I don't know what I'm talking about." She pulled away from him and started walking again.

He hurried to catch up with her. "You think I don't want to sleep with you?"

She laughed, a harsh little sound that held no humor. "I'm not that stupid. I'm a female with a pulse. I'd do, right?"

He pursed his lips. It was a low blow, but he could hardly argue with her. "I guess I deserve that. I've never pursued you because you're worth more than that."

She walked on in silence for a few moments, and then she stopped abruptly. Logan hadn't realized it, but they'd reached her house.

She gave him a sad smile. "I'd like to think that you're worth more than that, too."

The way she said it, the way she looked at him, he felt his heart swell in his chest. She made it seem like she really cared about him—and he had no idea what to do with that.

She unlatched the front gate then looked up at him. "Thanks for tonight. You're a good friend."

She was turning away from him, starting to walk down the path to her front door. He didn't want her to go, but he could only stand there watching.

She turned back when she reached the front door. "Goodnight, Logan."

"Wait a minute." He hurried down the path after her, and, when he reached her, he slid his arms around her waist.

"What are you doing?"

The honest answer was that he had no idea. He smiled. "What I've wanted to do for a long time." He slid his fingers into her hair and glanced at her lips before looking up into her eyes.

"Can I kiss you, Rox?"

A little sigh escaped her lips, and she sagged against him before she nodded. "Yes."

He pressed her back against the front door and closed his arm around her as she slid hers up around his neck.

Her lips were full and soft; they tasted so sweet as he ran his tongue over them. Her full breasts heaved against him as she hesitantly kissed him back. She sank her fingers in his hair, and all thoughts of restraint or finesse left his head. He crushed his lips against hers, and she opened up, letting him in as he claimed her mouth in a deep kiss that should leave no doubt about whether he wanted her.

When they finally came up for air, her cheeks were flushed, and her breath was coming deep and slow.

He ran his thumb over her cheek. "I'm sorry, babe; I couldn't resist."

"Don't say you're sorry. Phew! Wow." She blew out a sigh. "I'm going to go inside now, because otherwise I'll invite you to come in with me, and I think we'd both regret that tomorrow."

She was right. He knew it. He'd love to go inside with her, but he'd already told her she was worth more than just a quickie. "I can't disagree with you, but I can tell you I'd only regret it because this isn't the right way to start."

"Start what?"

"Start figuring out if we can take this somewhere."

She looked stunned. He felt stunned. He hadn't known he was going to say that.

"Where … where do you want to take it?"

He smiled. "You know I have no idea how this works. So, how about the first place we take it is for lunch tomorrow?"

She searched his face for a long moment.

"Before you ask me if I'm serious, I can tell you that yes, I am."

She smiled. "Okay, then. Lunch. Tomorrow. Call me."

Her smile filled his heart with hope. Though he didn't want to examine too closely what it was he was hoping for. He dropped his head and brushed his lips over hers. "I will. At ten-thirty. Now go inside before I try to persuade you to take me with you."

She laughed and opened the door. "You mean before I drag you in?"

He nodded emphatically. "Go. Quick. Close that door."

"Goodnight, Logan." She closed the door and left him standing there, staring at it.

He grinned and knocked.

"Yes?"

He laughed. "Are you still right there?"

"Yep. My knees are too much like jelly to go anywhere yet."

"Mine, too."

She laughed. "But you don't want me to open the door again?"

"Noooo! I want that more than anything, but it wouldn't be right. I'll see you tomorrow."

"Okay. See you then."

He couldn't help grinning to himself as he walked back the last few blocks to his house. This was a crazy idea. But it was one he couldn't resist.

~ ~ ~

Roxy stood with her back pressed against the front door for a long while, even after she heard the front gate click closed, and she was sure that Logan had left.

When she finally pushed herself away from the door, she made her way into the kitchen, where she poured herself a glass of water. She took a long cold drink and set the glass down.

Wow! That was the only thing her stunned brain could think. Wow, wow, wow! That kiss! She'd had an inkling that he'd be a good kisser—and that he'd be even better at everything that came after kissing—but nothing could have prepared her for the way he'd made her feel.

A shiver ran down her spine. She almost wished that her willpower had been a little less robust. He could be in her bed right now … but no. She needed to get a grip. She hadn't learned anything she didn't already know. Logan was gorgeous, the most attractive man she'd known in real life, and he knew how to kiss, and he knew how to turn a woman on. She'd already known all of that. She'd known it, but she hadn't experienced it before—and now that she had … No!

It had been a momentary lapse on her part—to be fair, she'd only gone along with it because he'd been so sweet about not wanting her to get hurt by her old friends. He'd taken her by surprise with how protective and thoughtful he'd been. But it was only a temporary glitch.

By next weekend, Lucy and the girls would no longer be here—and a whole new set of visitors would be. Logan would be back to his usual ways, and, hopefully, she'd have come back to her senses. Sure, she liked him, but so did pretty much every other woman who met him. She wasn't actively seeking a relationship, but when she embarked on one, it would be with a guy who wanted to explore something with her—not with a guy who wanted to explore every attractive woman who crossed his path.

She went through to the living room and sat down on the sofa; she was too wired to go to bed just yet. She jumped when her cell phone rang, and she pulled it out of her purse.

"Hello?"

"Hey, it's Angel. Are you okay?"

"I'm fine. What's up?"

"I just wanted to check on you. I didn't get to say goodbye before you left, and then I heard that you'd gone with Logan." Angel laughed. "I wasn't sure if I should call or leave you in peace."

Roxy chuckled. "If I was doing what you suspected, then I wouldn't have answered the phone, so you would have been fine either way."

"That's what I decided. So, he's gone? Or are you still with him?"

"He's gone. He walked me home, that's all."

"Oh, okay. I wondered if the two of you might …"

"For a minute there, so did I. So did he. But common sense prevailed."

"Are you glad?"

Roxy sighed. "I'm sure I will be by tomorrow. Right now, I'm sitting here wondering if I should have invited him in. On the one hand, I don't want to be just one more girl that he's slept with. On the other—why not be? What's the big deal? But then I remember; it'd make things too weird. He's a friend, one of the gang, and how would I feel every weekend watching him go home with another girl and another? I don't think I'd like that. He's a friend. And after tonight, he feels like even more of a friend."

"You don't think there's any chance you and he could be more than that?"

Roxy laughed. "Remember who we're talking about? I've never known him to see any girl for longer than a weekend."

"I know. I just thought that maybe the two of you might get together."

"I don't think so."

"Okay. Well, I won't keep you. I just wanted to make sure that you're okay."

"Thanks. I'm fine."

"I'm going into work in the morning, but I'll only be over there for a few hours. What are you doing? Do you want to meet up for lunch?"

Roxy smiled through pursed lips. "I can't."

"Why not?"

"I said I'd have lunch with Logan."

"Oookay. But there's nothing going on between the two of you?"

"Nope. I'm not even sure if he'll call to confirm like he said he would, but if he does, we'll have lunch. I think we probably need to make our peace and set things straight after tonight."

"What do you need to set straight? Did something happen between you?"

Roxy couldn't help the smile that spread across her face. "We might have kissed—just a little bit."

Angel squealed. "I like it! I think this is the start of something. I do."

"Don't get your hopes up. You sound like one of the voices in my head. Unfortunately, the other voice is louder, stronger, and more realistic. You know how he usually spends his Friday nights. He gave that up in order to go out of his way to help me out. A goodnight kiss is the least he deserved as a thank you."

Angel sighed. "If you say so. But I'm going to keep my fingers crossed that it meant more than that. I know you like him—and it seemed to me, and to everyone else tonight, that he likes you, too."

Roxy's tummy flipped over at the thought that he might actually be interested in her, but she came back down to earth with a bump. Even if he were, there was nothing that she would want to do about it. She hadn't had many boyfriends, but she knew that she wouldn't want to date someone like Logan.

"Aren't you going to say anything?"

"I don't know what to say, Angel. Yes, I like him, but it's a road to nowhere. I don't have the self-confidence to date a guy like him, even if he wanted to."

Angel blew out a sigh. "That's crazy talk, but it's late, and we don't know if it's pointless talk yet, anyway. But do me a favor, would you? After lunch tomorrow—whether you go with Logan or not—call me, and we'll meet up?"

"I'll call you, but I'm sure you have better things to do on your day off. I'll see you at work on Monday, anyway."

"If you don't call me, I'll call you."

Roxy smiled. "Okay. I'll call you. Now get off the phone and go tell Luke that I'm sorry you took so long. I'm sure he's waiting for you."

Angel chuckled. "You're right. I said I'd only be a minute."

"So, go. I'll talk to you tomorrow."

After she'd hung up, Roxy plugged her phone in to charge and made her way up to bed. As she brushed her teeth, she looked herself in the eye in the mirror. She wasn't bad looking, she knew that. She was no great beauty, but she had her good points. She'd never been the prettiest in her group of friends, and she knew she never would be. She wondered about that as she rinsed her face. Why did she believe that physical beauty determined the hierarchy of her circle of friends? In college, Lucy and Jana had been the prettiest—and the ones in charge. Lucy was kinder, and Jana was bossier, but they were unquestionably the leaders of the group. And they were the most popular with the boys.

Roxy continued to mull it over as she got ready for bed. Was it because the boys went after them that she saw them as somehow superior? And if so—why? It didn't make them any smarter, and it certainly didn't make them better people than her. She shook her head and turned off the light. For some reason, she'd allowed herself to believe that she wasn't as worthy as they were, and that was dumb. Was that why she didn't consider the possibility of her and Logan getting together to be realistic—because he was popular with the opposite sex and she wasn't? Did she think he was somehow better than her? No! She just knew that he wasn't the kind of guy to be satisfied with just one woman—and she wasn't the kind of girl who'd be happy to be one of many—no matter how well he might satisfy her!

Chapter Six

Logan rolled over and looked at the clock on his nightstand. Seven-twenty. Way too early to be waking up on a Saturday morning. He sat up. He missed the days when he used to be able to lie in bed and get back to sleep. He smiled as he got out of bed. If he was honest, it wasn't that often that he woke up in his own bed on a Saturday morning—or a Sunday for that matter—to be able to get back to sleep. And during the week, he was always up and out as soon as he woke up. There was so much to do at work.

He went downstairs and brewed himself some coffee, wishing that he hadn't let his thoughts stray toward work. There were a few things that he'd like to get done, but Nate had pretty much banned him from going in on Saturdays. In the early days, when Logan had first been brought in to turn things around, he'd practically lived on-site. He slept in his office more nights than he'd slept here at home. Things ran much more smoothly these days, and there was no need for him to put in the kind of hours that he used to. But still, whenever he had free time, his thoughts strayed to work and it wasn't usually too long before his truck took him in that direction, too.

He took his coffee upstairs. He had three hours before he could even call Roxy, and then it would probably be a couple more before she'd want to meet up. Now, in the cold light of morning, he was questioning the advisability of having lunch with her at all. Last night had been great. Especially that kiss on her doorstep. But that was the thing with kissing; it was only a precursor to what happened next. What happened next happened in bed. And taking Roxy to bed was a bad idea. There were friends, and there were fucks. It was an undeniable reality as far as Logan was concerned. Roxy was a friend— therefore, she couldn't be a … he couldn't … He shook his head to clear the images that were starting to form. Images of Roxy, her full breasts, her ample ass, her beautiful face. It was a bad idea. But it was one he couldn't shake.

He enjoyed her company too much to screw things up by complicating them. He only slept with women he was confident he wouldn't run into again. He saw Roxy all the time. He couldn't help smiling as he stepped into the shower. He'd like to see more of her. But what did that mean? He hadn't dated a girl in years. It got too complicated, they got too demanding, and there were so many of them passing through the resort here that there was no reason to get hung up on one girl in particular.

As he washed himself, it occurred to him that he *was* getting hung up on her. What he didn't understand was why. She'd been one of the gang—one of the guys almost, for a couple of years now. He'd always appreciated the way she looked, but he hadn't allowed himself to think of her as a woman—as a prospective partner—until just last night. And to him, a prospective partner was someone he wanted to sleep with, not someone he wanted to date, or to partner with for anything more than a weekend at most.

What he should really do was put her out of his mind. She'd sneaked into it in no time at all. He should be able to put her out of it just as quickly. He'd take himself to work. Get a couple of hours in and work all this craziness out of his system. By the time ten-thirty rolled around, he'd call her, tell her that he'd gotten caught up at work, and ask if they could have lunch some other time.

While he got dressed, he tried to convince himself that that was the best course of action. He'd gotten carried away. That was all. Last night he'd told Roxy that he wanted to see if something could happen between them. This morning he'd come to his senses. She'd understand. Hell, she'd probably feel the same way. She hadn't acted as though she was taking him too seriously. Apart from when he'd kissed her—and she kissed him back. Damn. He didn't need to be thinking about that kiss. He needed to get his ass in the truck and get himself to work.

When he got over to the offices at Four Mile Creek, he felt a bit better. Over here, everything was the way it always was. It was maybe better because there was no one around to harass him with questions or to derail him with urgent matters that he had to go help with. He managed to get a couple of hours done before he checked his watch. When he did, it was ten after ten.

He made a face and considered just not calling her at all. That would be easier. He could get back to work, get lost in what he needed to do, and just let ten-thirty roll on by. He stared at his screen again. He could do that. He pulled up the latest schedule that Aaron had been working on and started to check off expected delivery dates.

He only made it through three lines of the spreadsheet before he stopped to check his watch again. Ten-fourteen. Damn. He wasn't going to be able to do it. He'd told her he'd call her. It would be shitty of him not to. He'd call—and say he was at work; that wasn't a lie. He'd suggest they could have lunch some other time. That was open-ended enough, and they no doubt would have lunch sometime. It'd be with the rest of the gang and not the kind of lunch he'd meant when he'd suggested this, but still.

He stared at the screen again, but the numbers just floated before his eyes, refusing to make sense. He jumped when his cell phone rang. He stared at it for a moment before picking it up warily and checking the screen. Was Roxy calling him already?

Relief swept through him when he saw Zack's name.

"Hey."

"Where are you?"

"At work, why?"

"I was out for a run. I passed your place and didn't see your truck, and I wondered ..."

Logan smiled to himself. "Were you about to tear me a new one for doing something you I think I shouldn't?"

Zack laughed. "I was just curious."

"Well, I'm sure you'll be relieved to know that I walked Roxy home last night and said goodnight to her on her doorstep."

"I see."

"What does that mean? I thought you'd be pleased that I was a good boy."

Zack laughed. "I thought I would be, too. But I think I was kind of hoping that you were going to tell me that the two of you got together."

"Why?"

"I don't know. I thought the way you were so protective of her last night meant that you were finally ready to step up."

"Step up? What does that mean?"

"You know. Leave your childish ways behind and become a man."

Logan sat back. "You think my ways are childish?"

"No. It's just a turn of phrase. But then yeah, maybe. I mean you're playing a boy's game. All the sleeping around you do. At some point, you're going to … forget it. That sounds patronizing as hell, and that's not what I mean. Ignore me. I've been listening to the girls too much. Maria's got it into her head that you and Roxy are going to be the next pair to couple up. I'll be honest, I like the idea. I got so carried away with it that I forgot; you're you. It's not going to happen."

Logan thought about that for a moment.

"You still there?"

"Yeah."

"You mad at me?"

"A little bit. I'm more confused, though. I want to be pissed at you for calling me childish, but I know that's not really what you mean. It takes a man to step up and get into something real with a woman. I guess I am just a cowardly boy—I don't have the balls for it."

Zack laughed. "Sure, you do. You just haven't met the woman who makes you want it. For a minute there, I thought that things had clicked between you and Roxy. I guess I thought it'd be cool if the two of you got together. That's all."

"It's not that I don't like her."

"Hey, you don't need to explain yourself to me."

"I know, I think I'm trying to explain it to myself. See, last night I was thinking about something happening between her and me—and no, not just sex—but something more, you know? I'm supposed to take her to lunch today. See where it might go, but I've spent this morning talking myself out of it."

"Why?"

"Because that's not what I do."

"There's your answer then, right?"

"Maybe. But then again, maybe it's like you said—it's just not what I've done up until now; because I never met a woman who made me want to."

"And Roxy makes you want to?"

"I think so."

"So why not take her to lunch?"

Logan looked down at his watch. It was ten-twenty-nine. "Because I'd hate to get into something with her and let her down."

"There are never any guarantees. It's not as though she doesn't know what she'd be getting into. She knows who you are."

"That's true." He blew out a sigh.

"Why don't you have lunch with her and be straight with her? Tell her how you feel and tell her what you're scared of."

Logan laughed. "Admit weakness to a woman?"

Zack laughed. "Yeah, stop setting her up as this adversary from the opposite team and start seeing her the way you've always seen her—as your friend, and talk to her like one."

"But if she's a friend ..."

Zack laughed. "You're going to start in with your friends and fucks theory, aren't you? How about you think of it as friends with benefits—or better yet, becoming more than friends."

Logan pursed his lips.

"I think I've messed with your head enough for one day. Are you out tonight?"

"Probably."

"Okay. We'll be at the Boathouse later. You can tell me what you decided then."

"All right. I'll see you later."

After he'd hung up, he turned the phone over in his hands. Was he going to call her? He nodded and dialed her number.

~ ~ ~

Roxy stood in her laundry room, folding clothes. It wasn't often that she got a whole weekend off, but when she did, she liked to get all her chores out of the way early. She'd kept herself busy all morning telling herself that she was just taking care of the housework—not that she was trying to avoid thinking about Logan. She'd almost managed to convince herself that he wouldn't call. They wouldn't go to lunch, and last night would just be a slight deviation from course that they'd never mention again. Almost. She'd brought her phone with her, and it sat on top of the dryer—just in case. If he did call, she'd hate for him to think that she was avoiding him.

Even though she was staring at it while she folded a work blouse, she still jumped when it rang. Ten-thirty, on the dot. Her heart raced, and she stared at his name on the screen. Oh well. Here went nothing.

"Morning," she answered.

"Good morning. How you doing?"

"As well as can be expected for someone who's already on her second load of laundry on her day off,"

"Aww. I feel your pain."

Roxy smiled. She'd never thought about him doing laundry before. It made her feel a little closer to him for some stupid reason. "Are you doing the same?"

"Nah. I avoided it completely and came into work instead."

"Oh." She felt a ball of disappointment settle in her stomach. So, he was calling to say he wouldn't be able to make lunch.

"Are we still on for lunch?"

Her heart rate sped up again. "If you want, are you finished at work?"

"Yeah. I didn't need to come in. I was just … I … you know how it goes. Sometimes you just need to get stuff done."

"I guess. Don't let me put you out, though; we can do it another time if you're busy. It's no big deal."

"It isn't?"

She had to swallow before she answered. She'd kept telling herself since he left here last night that it was no big deal, that it couldn't be a big deal—and that to Logan it was probably nothing. She didn't know how to answer, so she turned the question back on him. "Are you saying it is?"

He was quiet for a long moment. She could hear the smile in his voice when he spoke again. "It's a deal. How big it is, we'll have to figure out. But … I dunno, Rox. Are you saying you'd rather forget about it?"

"No!" she said it before she could stop herself. "I don't know either, Logan. It's too weird for words."

He laughed. "It is, isn't it? I mean, who'd have thought … you and me?"

She was hardly about to tell him that she'd thought about it—a lot. "You're right, it's probably a bad idea."

"Maybe, but I say we should at least have lunch and talk about it. It'd be even weirder to just forget about it now. It'd make things awkward, and I'd never want things to be awkward between us."

"Me neither." She was starting to feel disappointed again. It sounded like he just wanted to smooth things over before they forgot about it.

"And besides," she could hear the smile in his voice again. "I'd like you to put my mind at ease about something."

"What?"

He chuckled. "I'll tell you when I see you. What time do you want me to pick you up?"

"Pick me up?"

"Yeah. There's no point in both of us driving."

"Okay. Whenever suits you. You're the one at work."

"How about noon?"

"Okay."

"Great. I'll see you then."

"You don't need to pick me up. I can walk."

"You don't even know where we're going."

"I don't? I assumed the Boathouse."

"Never assume. Especially with me. I'll see you at noon."

"Okay. Bye." Roxy hung up with a big smile on her face. How was it possible to go on such a roller coaster ride within the course of just a few short minutes like that? All she knew was that she was looking forward to seeing him—and to whatever he had in mind for lunch.

She ran upstairs and started going through her closet, trying to decide what to wear. She wanted to look good, but she didn't want to look like she'd gone to too much trouble. At least it was chilly out. She loved the late autumn. There'd been a light frost the last couple of mornings, and she loved frost—it gave a sparkly, magical quality everywhere—and more importantly, it gave her reason to dress in warmer clothes, that helped her cover the fact that she could hardly be described as svelte.

She flicked through the sweaters hanging in the back of the closet. She hadn't had many of them out since last year. She smiled when she reached a chocolate brown one that she loved. It looked good on her and covered her up without looking frumpy. She had a nice pair of brown boots that would go with it, and she knew exactly which jacket would look good with it, too. She breathed out a sigh of relief. It shouldn't matter how she looked. But it did. She didn't want Logan to see her and remember why he'd never shown any interest in her before.

She brought the sweater out and sat down on the bed. At the same time, she didn't want him to only be interested in the way she looked. Maybe this was a crazy idea. It would be pointless if she was going to spend the whole time second-guessing herself, and worse, second-guessing Logan and his motives. She pulled her favorite jeans out of the dresser draw and started to get changed. As she did, she gave herself a stern talking to. This lunch date might be something, and it might be nothing. It might solidify their friendship; it might be an exploration of something beyond friendship—or confirmation that there was nothing. But whatever it was going to be, she had to go into it knowing that she was good enough. Whether that meant good enough for him to be interested in her, or good enough to know that she was worth more than just another roll in the sack for him—whatever. She wasn't going to allow herself to get caught up in trying to be something—someone—other than herself just to get him to like her.

When she was ready, she checked herself over in the mirror. She looked good. She smiled. She looked happy and confident, and that was much more important than looking sexy or perfectly made up or whatever it was that men found attractive, but which few of them had ever seemed to find in her.

She did her best to stay busy until noon and tried to relax. It was only lunch. She tensed when she heard the doorbell ring, then smiled at herself. "Go do it. It's only Logan."

She chuckled as she made her way down the stairs. Only Logan? But it was true. Sure, she liked him, sure part of her had daydreamed about the sexy, popular Logan seeing something in her, but in reality, he was just a friend. Nothing about him made him any better than her. He was just as lucky that she would deign to spend time with him as she was that he'd want to spend time with her.

Her breath caught in her chest when she opened the front door. He was gorgeous! She might overuse that word when it came to him, but there was no other way to say it. His dark hair fell over one eye, his broad shoulders were encased in a denim jacket that she loved on him, and his smile … his smile lit up his eyes.

"Hey."

"Hi." She could feel herself smiling back.

He brought one hand around from behind his back and held out a single red rose. "For you."

"Thank you!" She took it from him with a shaking hand. "I didn't expect …"

He grinned. "Don't read too much into it. It just struck me on the way over here. You're supposed to give a girl flowers when you go on a date. I thought it'd be a nice gesture."

She took a deep breath and pulled herself together. He was right; she shouldn't read too much into it. It was probably a standard move for him.

"Come in a minute, let me put it in some water before we go."

He followed her through to the kitchen, where she kept her back turned to him while she found a vase and filled it at the faucet.

She tensed and froze when she felt him standing close behind her.

"Are you avoiding me?"

She turned around with a laugh. "Avoiding you? You're here in my kitchen, aren't you?"

"Yeah, but you haven't met my eye since I arrived."

Her heart was racing in her chest. She couldn't deny it, but she didn't want to admit it.

He put his hands on her shoulders and looked down into her eyes. "You can tell me now if you're just biding your time before you tell me that this is a bad idea?"

She shook her head, shocked that that was what he was thinking. "It's not that. I'm just a bit nervous, I guess."

He held her gaze for a long moment. "Nervous is one thing. Not interested is another. You're just nervous?"

She nodded.

His face relaxed, and he smiled. "Me too. I don't know what we're doing here, but I hope it's something. I just don't want you to feel you have to go along with it to be polite or something."

She laughed. "I wouldn't. I'd find it a lot easier to tell you I'm not interested than to …" She stopped, realizing that the only way she could end that sentence would be to tell him that she was interested.

He smiled, but to her relief, he didn't push her to explain. "Good to know. Shall we go, then?"

"Yeah, let's." She was eager to escape the confines of her kitchen and the need to examine what was going on between them.

Chapter Seven

When they were out in the truck, Logan glanced over at Roxy. She looked amazing. He couldn't remember a time she'd looked—or smelled—as good as she did right now. He had to wonder if his mind was playing tricks on him. She always looked good, but he didn't usually take it in the way he was doing now. He pursed his lips as he realized that up until last night, he hadn't seen her as anything more than part of the scenery of his everyday life. That was an awful thought. Why did he pay so much attention to women that he didn't know and overlook this beauty who was now, by some miracle, sitting beside him in his truck?

She gave him a puzzled look. "Is everything all right?"

He smiled. "I was just thinking that things couldn't be better. I'm glad we're doing this, Rox."

"Me too, but what exactly are we doing?"

His heart raced. He'd been hoping that over the course of their lunch, he might figure out just what it was he was doing. He was starting to consider all kinds of possibilities, but he wasn't ready to face them yet—let alone tell her about them. He hadn't expected her to put him on the spot this early on.

She made a face. "You made it clear that we're not going to the Boathouse, but where are we going?"

A wave of relief rushed over him. She only wanted to know where they were going to have lunch! That was a bit easier to answer. "Well, when was the last time you got out of town?"

"I don't know, not for weeks, probably months, now that I think about it. Why? What are you planning?"

"I thought we could go out Route Twenty, hit the mall, have lunch there and maybe do some window shopping. I thought it'd make a nice change."

She smiled. "And make it a bit easier to go unnoticed by prying eyes?"

"No! I'm not trying to sneak around if that's what you mean."

"Don't worry. If anything, I was thinking that way myself."

"You're ashamed to be seen out with me?"

"No. I just don't want to hear all the opinions about it."

He blew out a sigh and pulled the truck out into the street. "Yeah, sorry, I didn't think about that. It'll be easier for me— I'll hear how glad everyone is that I'm out with a nice girl like you. You'll get all the warnings about wasting time with a loser like me."

"You're not a loser!"

He chuckled. "I know. I just thought it was a better way to put it than admitting what people are really going to say if they think you've fallen for my wicked ways."

She smiled through pursed lips. "What do you think they'd say?"

He laughed. "That your virtue is at risk."

She laughed with him. "Who says I'm so virtuous?"

He shot a quick glance over at her. "I do, but I'd love it if you want to prove me wrong."

She shook her head. "I'm not going to play coy with you— after last night, you'd know it was a lie if I told you that I wouldn't want to ... prove you wrong. But ..." She shook her head. "I'm not good at being anything other than straight with people. I'm not interested in being just another girl you've slept with."

He nodded and kept his gaze fixed on the road ahead while he figured out how he should answer that. He wanted to be as honest with her as she was being with him, but that would mean admitting that he was thinking about whether there could be more between them.

He turned to her when she blew out a sigh. "Don't go all silent on me. If you're disappointed at me spelling it out like that, you should just turn the truck around. I don't want to waste your time if that's all you're looking for."

"It's not! I didn't answer because I don't know what to say. I'm tying myself up in knots here, Rox. I don't know what I'm doing, or where we're going. I want us to go somewhere, but I don't know how—what that looks like. You might need to help me out."

"I wouldn't know how. In case you haven't noticed, I don't have much experience with relationships. You're the expert."

He chuckled. "That's my point, I have next to zero experience with relationships. I don't do them."

She let out a harsh little laugh. "Come on, you're always ... oh! I see what you mean."

He nodded. "See. I can't deny that I get a lot of practice at one thing, but that doesn't make for a relationship. At least, not in my case. In my case, it's a way to avoid relationships."

"Why?"

He shrugged. "I can't say I've ever really thought about why before. I don't have some tragic past or a broken heart that's made me reluctant to get involved with someone. I just ..." Zack's words came back to him. "I never met anyone who made me want to. Till now."

He felt her turn to look at him when he added those last two words. He almost wished he could take them back, but he didn't. It was true, and he was starting to understand that the only way they were going to get anywhere was if he would follow her example and be completely honest with her.

"Why now?"

He laughed. "You need me to spell it out? Because of you. You're doing weird things to me."

He could tell she liked that, but she pressed on. "But I'll say it again; why *now*? We've known each other for a couple of years. I've never had this effect on you before."

"Haven't you?"

"I have? I'd never have guessed."

He shrugged. "You shoot me down pretty much every time I open my mouth. I know it's just banter, but you've never exactly been approachable. I didn't think you had the slightest interest."

"You didn't?"

"You did?" His heart was racing again. The way she said it sounded as though she was interested in him and couldn't believe that he didn't know it.

She gave him a rueful smile. "Of course! Have you ever met a woman who wasn't interested in you?"

"Ah." He was perfectly aware that he was blessed in the looks department. He'd spent most of his life using his looks to his advantage. Hearing that she liked him that way was nice, but it didn't mean much.

"I told you I haven't had much experience with relationships—in fact, now that I think about it, my behavior hasn't been much different than a grade-school kid with a crush. I like you, so I call you out on your behavior all the time."

He laughed. "Wow. That hadn't occurred to me."

"Me neither. But I can see it now. I'm like the quiet kid who has a crush on the popular boy, and who tries to hide it so no one—especially him—realizes and makes fun of her."

He turned to look over at her. "I'd never make fun of you, Rox. I wish I'd understood."

"Why? It would have just made things awkward—for both of us." She shook her head. "It probably still will. I mean, now you know, it'll be weird when we're all out, and you go off hooking up."

He shook his head slowly. "I won't."

She laughed at that. "Come on. It's who you are."

"It's who I've been. It was never who I planned to be for my whole life."

"Maybe, but you shouldn't pin yourself down to changing just because we're having a heart to heart."

"I'm not pinning myself down to it. I'm telling you it's what I want."

"Maybe it is, right now." She blew out a sigh. "We should probably slow this down. Who knows what's going to happen? We might hate each other by the time we get home this afternoon."

"Maybe." Logan had a feeling that, far from hating her, he'd like her even more than he did right now, even though that was hard to imagine.

~ ~ ~

"Do you want to have lunch first and then we can take a walk around afterward?"

"Sure." Roxy didn't know quite what to think about this little trip to the mall. She was glad that they weren't going to eat lunch at the Boathouse, where they'd be on full display for the whole town to see, and no doubt gossip about, but coming all the way out here almost made it feel as though they were sneaking around.

She climbed out of the truck and came around to meet Logan in front. He grinned at her. "I'm nervous, Rox. I don't know what I'm doing."

He looked almost boyish, and she had to smile. "I say we should just be us. We don't need to make a big thing out of it. We've been around each other enough in the past couple of years. We might not have done much, just the two of us, but it's no different than most weekends—we hang out and do something."

"I want it to be different, though." He offered her his hand.

She looked down at it for a moment and then looked up at him.

He gave her an earnest look. "You can refuse to hold my hand, and we can go in there as friends and just hang out like we always do. Or you can take my hand, and we can step into something new and different."

Her chest filled with warmth. She loved the idea of stepping into something new and different with him. She took hold of his hand with a smile. "Let's give it a go."

It felt strange to walk across the parking lot hand-in-hand with him. Strange, but good. His hand was big and warm wrapped around hers. It felt right. She glanced up at him, and he grinned at her. "I reckon we could get the hang of this, don't you?"

"Maybe, I like it so far, but there's a long way between holding hands and …" She didn't know what she meant to say.

"I know, but I have faith in us. We're smart, we'll figure it out."

She nodded. She'd love to figure out how to be a couple with him. But being a couple was about more than holding hands and making out. It dawned on her that she really didn't know him that well. She didn't know what was important to him—what his values were. All she knew was that he joked—and slept around—a lot. He was good to the people that he cared about, but he didn't seem to care about many.

He held the door open for her when they reached the mall entrance, and a blast of warm air ruffled her hair.

"Do you want to eat at Henri's?"

She nodded in surprise. She loved that place but thought of it as somewhere for a special evening meal, not just lunch.

He raised an eyebrow at her. "Why do you look so surprised? I thought you liked it there?" He pursed his lips. "Don't tell me, you thought I was going to treat you to lunch at the food court?"

She tried to hide a smile but didn't succeed. "In my defense, it is the mall. It's only lunch."

He shook his head. "True, but it's also our first date. Give me a little credit, would you?"

"Sorry." She did feel bad for underestimating him, but then she felt kind of justified, too. She hadn't realized that he saw this as a first date. When he'd arrived to pick her up, she hadn't been sure if this was just a lunch date to set the record straight about last night's wayward kiss.

"That's okay. I was about to ask how you could think so little of me, but it doesn't matter. All I need to know is that you do—and I need to show you who I really am."

"I'd like that. I think I've just painted you as the stereotypical …" She thought better of using the word she'd been thinking—manwhore.

He nodded. "I know. You don't need to say it. And I suppose it's fair. It's who I've been. I won't deny it. But it's not all I am. You'll see."

They'd reached the escalator, which would take them to the second floor where there was a row of upscale restaurants. He put his arm around her as they went up, and she let herself lean against him. She closed her eyes for a moment, enjoying the feeling. He was a big guy, solid. His presence felt reassuring. Standing there so close to him made her hope that this could go somewhere. She could happily get used to this.

Logan was surprised how much he enjoyed eating lunch with her. She was easy company, and she laughed a lot. He knew that about her, but he rarely got to experience her smiles and laughter directed at him. She joked around with their group of friends, but usually had a sharp word for him. He smiled at the way she'd described it—that she was like a little kid who had a crush and didn't know what to do with it.

He got to his feet when she returned to their table after visiting the ladies' room. "Do you want to go shop?"

"Sure. Do you need to get anything, or are we just browsing?"

He shrugged. "Just window shopping." He didn't need to buy anything, but he was hoping that she might spot something she liked, and he could buy it for her. He wasn't sure how the dating thing worked, but he knew that all girls liked gifts.

They spent the next hour wandering through the stores. She made him laugh with her observations about the people around them. When they came to the jewelry store, he tugged her hand and pulled her inside.

She gave him a puzzled look, but he just shrugged. "We've looked in every kind of store—why not this one, too?

She nodded and turned to look over the display of necklaces in the window beside her.

"Are you a jewelry kind of girl?"

"Not really. I have a few pieces that I wear, but not all the time."

He glanced at her ears, she was wearing little gold hoops, nothing fancy.

She smiled. "I do have some crazy earrings, but I save them for nights out."

It dawned on Logan that he'd never noticed her wearing crazy earrings—or any kind of jewelry, for that matter. It bothered him that he hadn't taken the time to notice details like that about her. The more time he spent with her, the more he liked her. He was enjoying walking around the mall with her much more than he'd enjoyed spending time with a woman in a long time. And that was saying something about her—in his mind, the mall didn't compare to the bedroom, and that was where he spent most time with women.

He watched her as she eyed all the trinkets that sparkled under the cleverly positioned lights. He loved that he could tell which ones she liked just by the expression on her face. She moved slowly along, looking at everything.

When she paused, and her eyes widened, he knew something had caught her interest, and came to stand beside her. "What have you spotted?"

She smiled and shook her head. "They're all so pretty."

"I know, but you just saw something that you really like."

She nodded. "You should probably know that I get sentimental sometimes. See that?" She pointed.

"Which one?" It was a display of necklaces with heart pendants.

"The battered one."

He laughed, understanding exactly which one she meant. It was silver and looked as though it had been hammered to give it what she so rightly called a battered appearance.

"My mom used to wear one after she and my dad got divorced."

He hesitated, not sure from the way she said it, whether her mom was still around. He didn't like to ask. He should know that about her. But he didn't.

She didn't notice his dilemma. She smiled. "She stopped wearing it after she met Ged. He's a good guy, they're married now, and happy. But I remember that battered heart of hers. I used to play with it when I was a kid. It just reminds me how strong she was and how she always used to tell me that hearts can take a hammering, but if they're full of love, they keep on beating." She gave him an embarrassed smile. "Sorry, that's probably too much information, but I love my mom. I'm so proud of how strong she always was for us when we were little, and happy for her that now she has Ged."

"Has she been with him for a long time? Was he part of your life growing up?"

"She met him in my senior year of high school. My dad left when I was eight. Mom had it hard raising us by herself."

Logan realized he didn't even know how many siblings she had. He'd heard those mean girls say that one of them liked her brother, but he didn't know if there was just the one. "How many of you are there?"

"Just me and my big brother. What about you? You only have older sisters, don't you?"

"Yeah. Three of them. Much older. I was an oops baby. I came along a lot later."

Roxy laughed. "An oops baby?"

He smiled. "You know—oops, we're pregnant again? They were supposed to be too old to have any more kids, and then I came along."

"I didn't know that." She frowned, and he guessed that she was feeling the same way he had a moment ago—wondering whether she should ask if his parents were still around.

"They live in Arizona now. In one of those oldie communities. They love it," he explained, to save her having to ask.

"It's weird that I don't even know that much about you. I knew you grew up here, and I'd heard you mention your sisters, but I'd never asked about your parents before."

"It's not so weird. You had no reason to know—just like I had no reason to know about yours. Till now." He looked at the necklace she'd been admiring. "Do you want it?"

She gave him a puzzled look.

"The necklace."

"Oh! No. That's sweet of you. But no. Even if I wanted you to buy me a gift—which I don't—I wouldn't want it to be a reminder of how much battering a heart can take."

He chuckled. "Yeah, sorry. I didn't think of it that way. You're right. I'd like to get you something, though."

She shook her head. "No. Thanks. It wouldn't feel right. Maybe if we get the hang of this and see each other for a while, you can get me something for Christmas."

He nodded, knowing that he'd screwed that up. "Or maybe just as a surprise, just because."

"I wouldn't say no to that either." She took hold of his hand and led him out of the store. "But for now, I'd rather have an ice cream."

He smiled as he followed her toward the food court, grateful that she was happy to gloss over the fact that he wasn't too great at this dating thing and its finer points.

Chapter Eight

Roxy stared out of the truck window on the drive back. The sky was gray and heavy, but she felt as though the sun was shining down on her. She was happy. Their afternoon out had been a lot of fun.

Logan looked over at her. "You'll get me paranoid, smiling away to yourself like that."

"Paranoid? About what?"

"You've got me thinking that you're really happy to be going home so you can get shot of me."

She laughed. "You couldn't be more wrong. I was smiling about what a nice day it's been."

He grinned. "Yeah? I'm glad you think so. I enjoyed it, too."

She nodded, wondering where it left them. She didn't have long to wonder.

"So, do you think you could stand to go out with me again?"

"Yeah, I think I could stand it if you can."

"I was thinking about tonight."

"Oh."

"You don't want to?"

"It's not that ... it's just. I didn't expect that." Her heart sank. She'd been so caught up in enjoying the moment she'd forgotten about reality. She hadn't been thinking ahead to what might—or might not—happen next.

"Well, it's Saturday night. We both usually go out with everyone. Do you want to go together?"

She nodded slowly.

"Is that a yes, or a not really?"

"It's a yes, but I'm wondering how it will work. What will everyone think—what will they say?"

"Does it matter?"

"Not really. I just … I guess I expect they'll be surprised."

"Probably, but I think they might like the idea. You'll get it much easier than I will—all you'll hear is that you need to be careful. I'll be the one getting all the ear-ache about how I'd better not mess up."

She smiled. "I can't argue with you there. But I'm more concerned about you messing yourself up."

"What do you mean?"

"Well, if we do this and then you change your mind and …" She wanted to let him know that she knew how he was.

"I told you. I don't want to keep playing the field. I want to …"

It was obvious to Roxy that he didn't know what he wanted. He liked the idea of exploring things with her, but it was uncharted territory for him.

He surprised her by reaching over and taking hold of her hand. "I like you, Roxy. You said this morning that we might hate each other by the time we got home today. I knew we wouldn't, but I wasn't prepared for just how much more I'd like you after spending a few hours with you."

He glanced over at her, and the look in his eyes took her breath away. He was usually so laid back, but now he looked determined. "I want to keep spending time with you. I'll no doubt screw up here and there, but it won't ever be intentional."

She smiled. "I know."

"What about you, though? How do you feel? Do you think there's enough between us to give this a try?"

She stared ahead for a long moment as he turned his attention back to the road. Did she? Yes, she'd liked him for a long time, but she'd never given any real consideration to whether she'd want to explore a relationship with him—because he was too much of a ladies' man. Now, he was asking her if she was interested, and she had to weigh whether she really was—and if she trusted him enough not to go straight back to his womanizing ways.

He squeezed her hand. "You don't have to answer right now. Think about it."

"I don't need to. I might be a fool, but I want to give it a try."

He grinned at her. "That's great."

"I hope it will be. But I warn you now, Mr. Perkins, if you jerk me around, you'll put our friendship at risk. So, maybe you're the one who needs to think about it. I'd rather not even try than have things go badly between us and mess up the way everything is now."

He squeezed her hand again. "I won't jerk you around, Rox, I promise. I'll be honest with you about everything."

She believed him. He might have been with a lot of women, but he wasn't what she'd call a player. He didn't string anyone along. He didn't tell women what they wanted to hear just to get them into bed—he told them he wanted to take them to bed, and it was up to them if they went. She knew most did.

A shiver ran down her spine. If this carried on the way it was heading, she'd go to bed with him, too. Part of her was excited at the prospect, but the little voice in her head was warning her to be cautious.

It was almost five by the time he pulled up in front of her house. "Do you want to come in?"

He held her gaze for a long moment before he shook his head. "I'd love to, but I've got stuff I need to do before tonight. If you still want to go with me?"

"I do."

"Okay. I'd better go and take care of my errands, and then I'll get ready. What time do you want me to come get you?"

"Whatever time works for you."

"Does eight work?"

"Yep."

"Okay. I'll be back here at eight."

"Okay." This felt weird. She'd thought he might come in with her when they got back. Memories of that kiss on her doorstep last night left her hoping for another one. But she could see her neighbors coming out of the house and walking up the path toward the truck. She didn't want them to see her kissing out here. Especially not kissing Logan. His reputation was well known around town, and she didn't want them thinking the worst of her.

She smiled at him and opened the door. "I'll see you at eight then."

He was leaning toward her, but she scrambled out of the truck quickly and opened her front gate. She didn't even look back in her attempt to avoid the neighbors.

By the time she'd let herself in and dared to go peek through the window, Logan was gone.

She laughed as she held up her hand to see how badly it was shaking. What kind of fool was she? What did it matter what the neighbors might think? What anyone might think. She'd cost herself a kiss, and probably confused poor Logan. But what the heck? If they were going to start seeing each other, there'd be plenty of kisses—and more—to come.

Logan slung his arm around Roxy's shoulders as they walked across the square toward the Boathouse.

She smiled up at him. "What are you smirking to yourself about?"

"Just that it feels good to be going in here with you." He didn't want to say that he liked the novelty of arriving here with a woman. Usually, he came alone but didn't leave that way.

She made a face, and he could tell she was thinking the same thing. He didn't want to start their night out on that note. He tightened his arm around her and stopped walking. She looked up at him again.

"What's wrong?"

"Nothing. I just want to make things a little bit righter before we go in there."

She smiled. "It'll be fine. You'll see. Angel called me when I got home. She wanted to know how this afternoon went. I think they all do. And from the sounds of it, they're all rooting for us to get together. They like the idea."

He searched her face. "Zack called me, too. I got the same idea. But I'm not worried about them and what they think. I'm concerned with what you think. I need you to know that I'm hopeful about us, Rox."

She smiled. "You are?"

"Yeah." He lowered his face to hers. It felt like the perfect moment. He wanted to kiss her. But he chickened out at the last moment and instead pressed his forehead against hers and looked into her eyes. She'd made a run for it rather than kiss him when he'd dropped her off earlier. Maybe it was too soon.

The look on her face told him that he should have gone for it, but it was too late now. The door to the Boathouse opened, and the sounds and smells of the busy restaurant filled the quiet square as a group of people came out.

He winked at her. "I want you to tell me how much hope you think there is after we leave here tonight." He stepped back and straightened his shoulders as if preparing to go into battle. "After we brave whatever they're going to throw at us." He held his arm out to her. "Are you ready to go do this?"

She laughed. "I am. Bring it on. We can handle it."

His heart buzzed in his chest when she said that. It sounded good to him—very good. He liked the idea that they could handle things together; that maybe, between them, they could handle anything life wanted to throw at them.

He took a deep breath as he held the door open for her to go in ahead of him. He needed to rein it in a bit. First, he needed to figure out how to handle spending a whole evening in the company of his friends and a … he smiled as the thought hit him … his girlfriend. She wasn't just a woman. She was his friend, and he was starting to hope that she would be his girl.

He followed her inside and took her coat as she shrugged out of it.

"They're over there." Roxy pointed to where the girls were sitting at a couple of the high-top tables.

He made a face. "I'm guessing the guys have gone to get the drinks in. What do you want? I'll meet you over there."

She laughed. "So much for let's go do this!"

He gave her a rueful smile. "I'm ready. I can do it. I just don't think it's wise to throw myself to the lions as a first step."

"You could have a point there." She looked over to where Maria, Angel, Amber, and Jade were not all staring at them.

"I'll take the first barrage of questions, but don't think that'll get you off the hook completely."

He laughed. "I don't. I just want to have a drink in my hand before I face them."

"Well, don't take too long about it. I need one, as well."

"Do you want a gin and tonic?" He knew that she liked those and was rewarded when she smiled and nodded.

"That'd be great, thanks."

As he watched her walk away, he realized that he was still holding both their coats.

"Want me to hang those up for you?"

He jumped when Ben, who owned the place, spoke beside him. "Jesus, Ben! You scared the crap out of me."

Ben laughed. "Sorry. I should have waited a minute. I could see that you were miles away."

Logan raised an eyebrow at him. "Are you going to be the first to warn me off?"

Ben shook his head. "Nope. The opposite, in fact. I've been waiting to see the two of you get together for a long time. Ever since you took over at Four Mile and wanted to use the conference room to start pulling the team together. Roxy went out of her way on every little detail to make sure that ran smoothly for you."

"She did?"

Ben smiled. "She did. And you're different around her, too. I'm not going to give you a hard time. There'll be enough people doing that. I just wanted to let you know I'm in your corner if you need me. I think it's a great idea."

That meant a lot to Logan. He respected the hell out of Ben, and hearing him say that he was in his corner made it feel like he was doing the right thing.

"Go get your drinks. I'll catch up with you all later."

Logan spotted Colt and Zack at the end of the bar but didn't make it to them before Kenzie, the bartender called to him.

"What am I getting you, big guy? It's on the house."

Logan grinned at her. If Kenzie was going to give him her blessing, then he felt like half the battle was won. "Thanks, Kenz! I'll take a beer and a G and T for Roxy."

She scowled at him. "These are from Ben, not me. I'll be watching you. And if you screw up …" She didn't need to finish the sentence.

He got the message loud and clear. Kenzie was not someone he'd like to piss off. No one in their right mind would. "I hear you, but how about you give me a chance? I like her a lot."

Kenzie's expression softened into a smile. "Aww. Don't get me wrong. I'm keeping my fingers crossed for you. But you need to know that if you mess with my girl …"

He held his hands up. "I know. I know! Believe me, I get it. I don't plan to do anything that could upset her."

Kenzie's scowl was back. "But you're a guy. Just because you don't plan to, doesn't mean you won't. Like I said, don't screw up." She set the drinks on the bar.

"Thanks."

She turned away to serve the people standing beside him, and Logan picked up the drinks and carried on to where Luke had now joined Colt and Zack, and the three of them were watching him.

"Okay. Before anyone says anything. Yes, Roxy and I are here together. And no, I don't plan to screw it up. Does that answer your questions and mean we can move on?"

Colt laughed. "Let me guess; Kenzie just read you the riot act and put you on the defensive?"

He nodded. "To be fair, I was already feeling a bit defensive. I don't know what I'm doing, and I don't need everyone getting on my case."

Zack grasped his shoulder. "We won't get on your case. We've got your back."

Logan shot him a grateful look. He didn't want to say anything sappy, but it was good to be reminded that these guys cared about him as well as about Roxy. They wouldn't give him a hard time just for the sake of it.

Chapter Nine

"Where's Austin tonight?" asked Jade.

Roxy shrugged and looked at Colt. He was the most likely to know.

He shrugged, too. "I left him a message when I got off work, but I haven't heard back from him. Maybe he wanted a night in. I know he's been busy lately."

Logan grinned. "He has. He's presold four of the new builds at Four Mile in the last couple of weeks, and that's aside from all his regular listings."

"Do you think we should text him and make sure he's okay?" asked Maria. She was like the mother of the group in some ways, always keeping tabs on everyone and caring about them all.

Colt nodded and pulled his phone out of his pocket. "I planned to do that when I got here." He grinned at Logan. "But I forgot when we all got started grilling you."

Logan laughed, and Roxy felt her cheeks color up when he put his arm around her shoulders. "Yeah. I'm glad we got that out of the way. And now you all know that I'm wooing our Roxy here. I'm hoping that instead of giving me a hard time, you'll give me some pointers when I look like I might screw up."

"Aww," Maria caught Roxy's eye. "I'd say he's doing very well, so far. Though the important thing isn't what any of us think. It's what you think. How's he doing?"

Roxy kept a stern face and turned to look at him. She couldn't keep it up when she saw the panic in his eyes. It made her laugh. "Jeez, you're going to have to find your sense of humor again, Perkins. I was only going to pull your leg."

He narrowed his eyes at her. "You almost gave me a heart attack. I thought I'd screwed up already, and I had no idea how."

She laughed and rested her head against his shoulder for a moment. "Nah. You're fine."

Zack grinned at him. "I wouldn't worry about that. I get the feeling that when you do screw up, you'll hear all about it straight away. Right, Rox?"

She laughed, but it made her feel icky. She didn't want to set things up along the lines of Logan being on trial and her being ever ready to call him out or set him straight. Her smile faded as she realized that that had, in fact, been the dynamic of their friendship up until this point. She'd always made sure that she let him know how much she disapproved of his ways. She turned to look at him, and he smiled.

"Do you want to dance?"

"Sure."

They made their way out onto the dance floor, and he slid his arm around her waist, drawing her closer as the band started playing a slow ballad.

She laughed and looped her arms up around his neck. "Was this deliberate?"

"What?" He gave her an innocent look, but she could see the laughter in his eyes.

"You brought me out here just in time for the erection section."

He laughed and looked down at the couple of inches of space that he was keeping between their bodies. "I was hoping you wouldn't remember that."

Her heart started to race. She was confused. Did he mean that he was keeping his distance so that she didn't notice, or that he didn't have ... didn't *feel* that way about her and was hoping that she wouldn't remember that he should?

"What's wrong?"

She shook her head. "Nothing."

He hooked two fingers under her chin and made her look up into his eyes. Damn. They were beautiful eyes—big brown ones that she could happily get lost in. Except not right now. Right now, she was too busy trying to avoid them so that she wouldn't have to admit that she was freaking out about whether he was even attracted to her.

"Come on, Rox. You just went stone-cold on me."

"Sorry. I ... you ..." She looked down at the space between them again. "I don't understand what you meant. This is the erection section, but the way you're keeping me at arms-length tells me that it's not—not with me."

His eyebrows knit together. "What do you mean?"

"It doesn't matter. Forget it. I was just being stupid."

He continued to search her face as if he might find the explanation there. Somehow, it seemed that he did. Under other circumstances, it would have been comical to see the change in his expression when the light came on for him. He shook his head in disbelief. "You think I'm keeping you at arms-length because I'm not ... feeling it for you?"

She shrugged and wouldn't meet his eye. She felt really stupid now and wished that they'd just let the moment pass. She shouldn't have said anything.

His closed both arms around her waist and pulled her close against him. A wave of heat rushed through her as her breasts pushed against his chest. Their bodies touched from the knees up—and if she'd needed reassurance as to whether he was attracted to her that way, she now had it—in a big way.

A sigh escaped her lips before she could stop it. He held her gaze and looked deep into her eyes. "Does that help?"

She ran her tongue over her bottom lip and nodded, not trusting herself to speak.

"Good. You'd be crazy to think that I don't feel that way about you, Rox. I just didn't want to scare you off."

She bit her bottom lip. Scary wasn't the word that came to mind for her.

"I'm trying to do this right. I know what you think of me, and I don't want you to think that's all I want. I can wait."

She pressed her lips together. He might be able to wait, but the way he was still swaying her to the music and the way her body was reacting to the hard proof of his attraction pressing into her, she wasn't sure she could!

The song came to an end, and she took his hand and led him off the dance floor. The poor guy was trying to do the right thing. She didn't want to make it any harder for him. She had to bite back a slightly hysterical giggle at that thought—he was already hard enough.

"That was easier than I thought it'd be," Roxy said as they made their way out at the end of the night.

"It was," Logan agreed. "None of the girls gave you a hard time when I wasn't around?"

"No. They like the idea. They think it'd be kind of cool if we were together. I used to hang out with Maria and Angel all the time, but now that they're with Zack and Luke, it's different."

He raised an eyebrow at her.

"Not in a bad way, just different. They do coupley things. It's no fun being the fifth wheel."

"Yeah. I can see that." He put his arm around her shoulders as they walked across the square. "Do you think it'd be cool if we were together? Would it make it easier for you to hang out with your friends?"

She looked up at him. "It's not about that."

"I know. I don't know why I said it." They walked on in silence for a little while. "Actually, I said it because it's easier than asking if you like the thought of us being together just for the sake of it."

She smiled. "I know. We're both tiptoeing around the edges here. So, I'll wade in and put myself out there first. Yes. I do like the thought of us going out together. I like you."

He felt relieved and like an asshole at the same time. He wasn't a coward—usually. "I like you, too, Rox." He hadn't meant to make her be the first to put herself out there. He didn't want her to feel that she had to take the lead. He might not have a lot of experience at this—but he wasn't a pussy. "In fact, I was asking because I was wondering …" He almost stopped and changed course, but if they were going to do this, he needed to go all in. "Do you want to be my girlfriend?"

She stopped walking and looked up at him. Her expression was the same as it had been this afternoon when she'd seen that battered heart necklace in the jewelry store. It made his heart buzz. He knew her answer before she spoke.

"Yes. I would. I'd like that a lot." She chuckled. "I don't know if people our age ask each other to be boyfriend and girlfriend—it seems like a kids' thing. But I'm glad you did."

He grinned back at her. "I know. It sounds a bit cheesy, but I'm new at this. From what you've said, we both are. You were mean to me because you liked me. I'm asking you to be my girlfriend. Maybe we are both like kids, but we can grow into it."

She pushed at his arm. "I wasn't mean to you. I just call you out on your shit—and that isn't going to stop."

He laughed and carried on walking. "Fair enough. So, you're not going to be that girl who hangs on my every word and agrees with everything I say?"

"Ha! You already know the answer to that one. And if that's what you're looking for, you've come to the wrong place."

"Oh, believe me. I'm fully aware of that."

Just like last night, they reached her house all too quickly. He didn't want the evening to end, but he knew it had to. He didn't want to rush into bed with her—well, he did, but he didn't think she'd want to. And part of him was still hung up on it. Sleeping with a woman normally meant that he wouldn't see her again—not that it was the beginning of something. With Roxy, that was exactly what he wanted it to be. To his surprise, that made him nervous.

She opened the gate and raised an eyebrow at him. "What happens next?"

He chuckled. "I was just asking myself the same thing. What do you want to happen?"

He loved the way she tried to hide her smile but didn't manage it. "I'm not sure I should say. I think you know, but I'm not sure it's a great idea."

He nodded sadly. For a moment there, he'd been ready to throw caution to the wind. "It's probably not. Not yet. What are you doing tomorrow?"

She shrugged. "Not much."

"Want to hang out again?"

She smiled. "I'd love to."

"Okay." He was surprised that his heart was hammering in his chest. He'd never felt so conflicted about what should happen at the end of the night. Usually, it was a foregone conclusion. This should be a foregone conclusion that he should let her go to bed alone, but he couldn't make himself want to walk away.

He put his arm around her shoulders and walked her up the path to her front door. She was feeling it too; he could tell. Her eyes sparkled, and her breath was coming slow and shallow.

He put his hands on her shoulders and looked down into her eyes.

She dropped her gaze.

"Remember, I told you I wanted you to put my mind at ease about something?"

She looked up. "About what?"

He smiled. "I wanted to ask if it was okay that I kissed you last night."

She nodded. "It was."

He lowered his lips toward hers and stopped just a couple of inches away. "And would it be okay if I do it again?"

She nodded almost imperceptibly as he closed his arms around her waist and drew her against him. It was a bad idea. The feel of her soft, warm body pressed against him did nothing to strengthen his resolve to walk away.

Her arms came up around his neck, and her full, soft lips met his. He started out slowly, not wanting to scare her off—or to give in to his instincts and kiss her senseless until she had no choice but to take him inside.

She kissed him back, tentatively at first, but she soon picked it up, opening up to him, kissing him hungrily, until he had to lift his head. She was driving him crazy with need for her.

She gave him a sad smile, apparently believing that he was being the one with the self-control. "You're right. I should go inside; you should go home." She blew out a sigh. "But you'd better go quick before I drag you in with me. Last night I talked about it; tonight, I might just do it."

He closed his eyes for a moment. She was trusting him to be the responsible one. It took everything he had, but he nodded slowly and then planted one last kiss on her lips. "Get inside while you still can. I'll call you at ten."

She searched his face, and he wondered if she was going to ask him to come in. He wouldn't be able to say no if she did.

She winked at him. "Thank you for being stronger than I am. Goodnight, Logan."

"Goodnight, Rox."

He watched as she opened the door and stepped inside, then he leaned against the porch when she closed it behind her. Damn. Here he was out in the cold for the second night in a row—and he was proud of himself!

"Are you still out there?"

He chuckled when her voice came through the door. "I am, but I'm about to make myself leave—before I kick your door down and come in there to get you."

She laughed. "Ooh. I like the sound of that."

He shook his head. "Don't tempt me, Rox. I'll see you tomorrow."

He heard her heave a big sigh. "Okay. Goodnight."

Roxy couldn't believe it when she opened the curtains on Sunday morning and saw everywhere coated with a hard frost. The sun shone down and made everywhere look sparkly and beautiful, but she'd been hoping for a warm day. She'd had visions of going for a walk with Logan, getting to know him better. She couldn't help but smile at the thought—her boyfriend! She hadn't had one of those since college. Sure, she'd dated a little, but nothing serious.

She went through to the kitchen to see if the coffee was ready. Serious wasn't a word she'd thought she'd ever use about Logan, not with any woman, and especially not with her. It was probably still too soon to use it, too soon to say whether it might turn into something serious. She wasn't even going to allow her mind to go near the question of whether she wanted it to.

She was just going to enjoy it for what it was, for however long it lasted. Today, that meant hanging out together again. She hoped the weather would cooperate. If it was too cold, they could do something indoors. She pressed her lips together as she poured herself a mug of coffee. The only trouble was, there was one obvious thing they could do together indoors, and as much as she wanted to, she wasn't sure that she wanted to do it yet.

He'd been so sweet last night—and the night before. If he'd made any attempt to persuade her, she would have given in. She had no doubt about that. But he'd respected her, and that meant a lot. She knew she'd be feeling a lot less confident about the two of them if they'd started out with a bang, so to speak.

When he did call, a little while later—at ten, just like he'd said—she was both nervous and excited about what he suggested. He wanted her to come over to his place. She'd been there a couple of times, but always as a part of a group. She hadn't been alone with him before.

He'd said that he'd come pick her up again, but she'd told him that she'd walk. It was sweet that he liked to do that, but if they were going to start seeing each other, he'd have to get used to the fact that she liked to walk as much and as often as she could. She sat on her ass most of the time at work. So, in her free time, she liked to get out and about for the fresh air and the exercise.

She'd said she'd be there around noon, and she set out ten minutes early so that she could take a detour down by the lake. She loved to see the water on frosty days like this, and she had a feeling that she and Logan wouldn't be venturing out.

She stopped when she passed the parking lot that served the public beach. There were only a couple of cars there. She considered going down to the beach, but she didn't want to take the time. She'd be able to see the lake for most of her walk, and not only was she in a hurry to see Logan, but there was a cold wind whipping off the water.

She walked on and watched as a group of people got into one of the cars and pulled out of the lot. The car slowed as it passed her. She expected it to be tourists asking for directions but was surprised to see Jana roll the window down and wave at her.

"Hi, Roxy."

"Hey, girls." Roxy felt bad that she hadn't given them another thought since she'd left the Boathouse on Friday night. "I hope the party went well?"

Lucy leaned forward so she could see her from the driver's seat. "Thanks, Roxy. It was a good time. I'm sorry again that I didn't invite you."

"There's no need. It was nice to see you. I hope the wedding goes well."

"Thanks. I'll send you photos."

Roxy nodded, knowing that she probably wouldn't and that it didn't matter. When she'd first seen Courtney at the lodge, she'd felt a little hurt and left out. Now, she was over it. Life had moved on—hers and theirs. She was better off not keeping in touch with them. The friends she'd made here were much better friends—better people. She didn't feel like a second-class citizen here.

She waved as the car pulled away. It seemed fitting, as though their departure marked that part of her life as being over, just as she was on her way to Logan's house, hopefully, to embark on a new chapter.

~ ~ ~

Logan had been watching the driveway since ten before twelve. He still wished she'd let him go pick her up. He checked out the window again and then looked around the kitchen. Everything was clean and tidy—not that that was unusual for him. He took good care of the place. Growing up with three older sisters might have made some men spoiled and unable to take care of themselves. That wasn't the case for him. His sisters had taught him how to do for himself and not just the basics. He'd done his own laundry for as long as he could remember—and that included sewing and mending, too. He loved to cook, and he liked to keep his place clean. He smiled as he checked the spinach dip in the oven—five more minutes. Up until now, he'd thought of all those skills as necessary, but not something he'd ever brag about. Now, he was hoping to impress Roxy with just how domesticated he was.

He felt a big grin plaster itself across his face when he looked out of the window and saw her. Damn, she was beautiful. She looked up at the house as she made her way up the drive. He could tell that she liked it. For some reason, that made him like her all the more. He loved this house. It was old and full of character. He might build new houses, but he didn't love them the way he loved this place. He was glad that Roxy seemed to appreciate it. He didn't want her to be one of those girls who liked everything modern and soulless.

He went to open the front door and stepped out onto the porch. "Come on in, it's freezing out here."

She trotted up the steps and greeted him with a smile. Her cheeks were pink with the cold, and she looked even more beautiful than she had yesterday. He was starting to think there was some kind of magic going on; the more he looked at her, the more beautiful she became. It was the opposite of what happened with the women he usually went out with.

When she reached the top, he wrapped his arms around her and dropped a peck on her lips. "Come inside, let's get you warmed up."

She tried to hide a smile, and he had to wonder if she'd picked up on the ambiguity of his words at the same time that he had. He'd love to get her warmed up and come inside. He bit the inside of his cheek as he closed the door behind them. He'd set himself the challenge of trying to get through this afternoon without getting physical.

As he took her coat from her and hung it on the coat stand in the hallway, he had a feeling that might be a challenge that he wouldn't be able to meet.

Chapter Ten

"Thanks," said Roxy as she took the beer that Logan handed her. It was sweet that he'd bought wine for her, but they'd spent the afternoon watching football, and football called for beer.

He grinned as he sat down beside her. "I told you, you wouldn't beat us."

She made a face at him. "If it hadn't been for that dumb call, you wouldn't have made that last touchdown."

He laughed. "Note to self: she's a sore loser, don't rub it in."

"Hey!" She pushed at his arm. "I am not a sore loser. I just hate to see the better team lose because of a bad call."

He narrowed his eyes at her. "Did you just claim that the bunch of clowns that you call a team is better?"

She nodded emphatically, trying to hold back her laughter. "You know they are."

"I know no such thing, and I need you to take that back."

"Ha! There's no way I'm taking back the truth."

He leaned toward her until their noses were almost touching. "Take it back."

"Or what?" Her heart was racing. This was the closest that he'd come to her all afternoon. The tension had been zinging in the air between them, but she'd been grateful that they'd kept themselves distracted by watching the game and bickering over their teams.

Any chance of distraction disappeared as he took her beer from her hand and set it down on the coffee table. He set his hands on either side of her hips and leaned forward until she had to lean back on the cushions.

"You want to know what I'm going to do if you don't take it back?"

The way her body was reacting to this closeness, she could barely even remember what it was he was talking about. All she was interested in was what he was planning to do.

He lowered his lips toward hers. "I may have to kiss you."

She smiled and looked into his eyes. "In that case, there's no way I'm taking it back."

His lips came down on hers, and as if they had a will of their own, her arms came up around his neck, pulling him closer. She loved the way he kissed her. Up until now, his kisses had started out tentatively and followed her lead. Now, he was less restrained. He claimed her mouth with his own, and she responded hungrily.

She was disappointed when he finally lifted his head. She'd told herself on the way here that it was too soon to give in to her desire for him. But lying next to him on the sofa like this, it felt like it couldn't happen soon enough.

He looked down into her eyes and smiled. "Sorry, Rox. I got a bit carried away there."

She reached up and touched his cheek with a rueful smile. "Don't say sorry. I did too. It's not like you had to work hard to persuade me or anything, is it?"

He chuckled. "No, but I was prepared to."

She raised an eyebrow at him. "How hard were you prepared to work?"

"Honestly? As hard as necessary." He rocked his hips against her. "Does that give you any idea how hard?"

Ripples of excitement coursed through her as she felt just how hard he was. She reached up and cupped his face between her hands. "Is it what you want?"

He turned his face to one side and kissed the palm of her hand. "I think you already know the answer to that. However, what's more important is whether it's what you want."

"I think you know the answer to that, too."

His smile faded, and he looked serious. "It's easy to say that it's what you want in the heat of the moment. But would you be happy about it afterward? The trouble is, I don't know if you can answer that question until afterward, and so I guess that part of me is trying to put afterward off for as long as possible."

"Are you saying you think we should wait?"

"I think I am, but I don't want to."

Roxy couldn't help but feel disappointed.

"Hey, don't look like that. This is me trying to show that I care about you."

"I know, and on the one hand, I appreciate it. On the other, it doesn't make me feel great."

Logan sat back and pulled her up to sit beside him. He put his arm around her shoulders and looked down into her eyes. "I'm sorry I'm screwing this up. I want to make you feel great." He waggled his eyebrows at her. "I'd love to make you feel great in every sense. I'm holding back because I don't want you to think that's all I'm interested in. And, if I'm honest, I have a bit of a hang-up about myself."

She gave him a skeptical look. "I didn't think you were someone who had many hang-ups."

"Not like that. What I mean is… This is going to sound dumb, but it's kind of that I respect you too much."

Roxy searched his face. It seemed that he was absolutely serious, and that surprised her. She almost asked if he didn't respect the women he usually slept with, but she thought better of it.

She got to her feet. "Well, the moment has definitely passed for now. What do you say, do you want to go out for a walk?"

He stood to join her. For a moment, he looked like he was about to argue, but his face relaxed, and he smiled. "Yeah. I'm sorry I screwed this up, a walk might help reset things."

Roxy was relieved to be out in the fresh air. She was still struggling to decide how she felt about him holding back like that. She wanted to be glad that he would rather take it slow, but at the same time, she couldn't help but feel disappointed.

He took hold of her hand as they walked the short distance to the end of his street. Instead of turning the corner to follow the path toward town, he led her down another path that disappeared into a stand of trees.

She looked up at him with a smile. "Where are we going?"

"You'll see in a minute."

And indeed, in just a few minutes, they emerged on the other side of the trees, and to her surprise, they were standing on a long thin stretch of beach.

"Wow! I didn't even know this was here."

"Not many people do. I've been coming down here since I was a kid. It's like my own private beach most of the time. I'm usually the only one here, but I don't mind sharing it with you." He leaned down and dropped a kiss on her lips.

"Aww, aren't you the sweetest?"

He swaggered his shoulders. "I'm doing my best."

They walked in silence for a while along the water's edge. It was getting colder, and the sky almost had the look of snow.

"Are you okay?" asked Logan. "Do you want to go back?"

"Not yet. It's so pretty out here. Unless … Are you cold?"

"I'm fine. I was just thinking about you."

"Do you come down here often?" She hadn't thought of him as being the kind of guy who would come down to the beach by himself.

"I do. I try to get down here most days, either before work or afterward. It's peaceful. It helps me clear my mind."

Roxy hadn't ever thought of him as someone who had so much on his mind that he needed to clear it. "Is work stressful?"

"It can be, but I love it. I landed on my feet when Nate offered me the job. It's a lot of responsibility, but I enjoy it."

"What did you do before?"

"I paid my dues. I went down to LA and worked in construction there."

"Wow. I didn't know that. I thought you'd always lived here. What made you come back?"

"I missed the place. I wasn't made to live in the city. This is my home; it's where I'm from, where my people are."

"Your people? How many of your family are still here?"

"Like I said, my folks are in Arizona, one of my sisters lives in the city, she was the one who helped me find work down there, but my other two sisters are still here."

Roxy nodded, surprised that she hadn't even known that about him. "Is it weird that we've hung out so much over the last couple of years and yet know so little about each other?"

"I don't think so. We've only really connected through our group of friends, and most of them don't have family here. In fact," he grinned at her, "most of you are imposters."

She laughed indignantly. "You think of me as an impostor?"

He slung his arm around her shoulders. "No, not really. I'm glad you're here. But you only came here for the job at the Lodge, right?"

"I did. I guess I'm like you. I'm not made for the city either. I was working at a big hotel in LA, but I was miserable. I'd been up here a couple of times for weekends away, and when I saw that they were advertising for people to work at the Lodge, I applied straight away. I already knew I loved it here."

"Was it a smart career move for you?"

She gave him a puzzled look. "I don't suppose it was. I was in the fast-track management program in LA. I could have worked my way up and done well. It's different here. Angel is the general manager, and I'd guess that she'll be here for life. That means the most that I can aspire to is to be her second-in-command. So, as far as a career move goes, it probably wasn't the smartest. But as far as I'm concerned, it was a great life move."

He stopped walking and slid his arms around her waist, pulling her against him. There was no mistaking the desire in his eyes as he looked down into hers, but there was something else in them, too. Something she didn't understand.

"I hope it was."

She gave him a puzzled look.

"I hope that coming here will turn out to be a great life move for you."

A shiver ran down her spine. She didn't want to let herself believe that he meant what she thought he did. It sounded like he was talking about them getting serious. But she was probably just letting her imagination get carried away. Him asking her to be his girlfriend was as serious as it got for him. She knew that.

She sagged against him as he cupped the back of her head with his hand and claimed her mouth in a deep, slow kiss. She snuggled closer against him, wanting to feel the warmth of his body—and hoping he might get the message about just how much he was heating hers up.

He lifted his head and searched her face. "I want you, Rox, but it's up to you. We should head back to the house. It's too damned cold out here, but when we get there, I need you to decide if it's time for you to go home."

She held his gaze for a long moment. Her mind was struggling to remember all the reasons that it would be better to go home. Her body wasn't interested in whatever those reasons might be. Instead, it was straining to get closer to his, feeling as though waves of electricity were zinging through her, zipping from her taut nipples that were crushed against his chest down to the place between her legs where the heat and anticipation were building.

"I understand if you say you want to leave."

She shook her head slowly. "I don't."

He smiled and turned her around to face the way they'd come, then stood behind her and wrapped his arms around her waist, marching her back toward the trees.

She laughed. "What are you doing?"

Shivers chased each other down her spine when he spoke next to her ear. "Taking you straight home before you change your mind."

Chapter Eleven

Roxy looked nervous when they got back to the house. Logan took her coat and hung it in the hallway next to his. He closed his arms around her and hugged her to his chest. All the way back, he'd had visions of undressing her right here in the hallway just as soon as they made it through the door. Now that they were here, he knew he had to take it slower than that. She was tense, and that wasn't how he wanted this to go.

"Do you want another beer?" he asked.

"I thought …" Her cheeks flushed, and she didn't meet his gaze.

He rested his chin on top of her head and hugged her closer. "Are you in a big hurry? I didn't realize you wanted to go straight at it."

She chuckled. It felt good to feel her move in his arms like that. She was relaxing.

"Don't worry. I haven't changed my mind, but I'd rather just let it happen. Now that we're back here, now we know we both want it to, I imagine it'll just develop naturally." He winked at her. "Unless you're the kind of girl who prefers a set schedule? Five-ten get back to the house. Five-twenty, clothes are removed. Five-twenty-five, insert tab A in hole B?"

She laughed and slapped his arm. "No. That isn't what I had in mind. You're right. Now that we've cleared the air, we can just relax and see what happens. So, yes, I would like a beer."

He went to get them from the fridge and stopped in the doorway to the living room on his way back from the kitchen. She'd taken a seat on the sofa and had her legs curled up beside her. She looked relaxed, at home—his heart thudded to a halt; she looked like she belonged here!

She met his gaze with a smile. "What's up? Am I not supposed to put my feet on the furniture?"

He came in and set the drinks on the coffee table. "I was just taking in the beauty."

She rolled her eyes. "You don't need to bullshit me. I've already told you that I'm …" She dropped her gaze, looking embarrassed. For some reason, that turned him on. He was used to women who openly told him what they wanted. Her hesitation was so much sexier than that.

He raised an eyebrow as he sat down beside her. "That you're what?"

Her lips quivered into a smile. "You know, you don't need to make me say it."

"Maybe I want to hear you say it." His cock strained in his pants, dying to hear her say that she wanted him.

"You don't need to say all the right things to get me to sleep with you; that's what I mean." She picked up her drink and took a big gulp. "Though, I might need a bit of Dutch courage."

"I'm not trying to say the right thing, Rox. I'm telling you what I see. You're beautiful."

She shrugged. "I'm okay. I'm not exactly your usual type, though, am I?"

He didn't want to go there. He didn't want to talk about the girls who were his type—especially since that had more to do with their willingness than their looks.

"Come on, I'm not a small girl, we all know that. You usually go after model types, pretty faces, perfect bodies."

He needed to make her stop. He couldn't stand to hear her compare herself unfavorably to the girls he hooked up with. That was all they ever were—hookups. He put his arm around her and moved her so that she was sitting with her legs across his lap. "They might be pretty, but you're beautiful." He allowed his fingertips to graze the side of her breast and felt her body react to the slight touch. "You have the perfect body. Perfect for me."

She looked up into his eyes. He'd half expected her to protest, but she didn't, so he continued, allowing himself to rest his hand on her thigh and slowly move it up. "You're gorgeous, Rox. Don't go thinking that I didn't want you from the first time I met you. The only reason I didn't do anything about it was because you were too real. You called me out on my shit right from the get-go."

She nodded. "I'm not calling you out on it now."

"I'm not feeding you shit. I'm telling you the truth." He leaned closer and sucked her bottom lip. "Whether you believe me or not."

Her arms came up around his neck. "I want to believe you."

He nodded and nuzzled his face into her neck as he spoke again. "It'll take time, I get that. I don't mind. I'll show you, time and time again." He trailed his tongue over her collar bone and loved the way her breasts heaved in response.

"You mean that, don't you?"

He hadn't expected her to question him again, and he smiled when she did, moving his hand farther up her thigh as he nipped at her neck. "I do, but I'm getting the impression that words aren't going to be enough to convince you."

Her fingers tangled in his hair as he kissed his way down between her breasts and finally allowed himself to close his hand around one of them.

"Oh," her voice was low and breathy.

"I think I need to show you."

"I think you do."

He looked up into her eyes and was pleased to see that they were glazed with lust. He had a feeling that they matched his own.

She cupped his face between her hands and brought him up to kiss her. The hunger with which she kissed him back urged him on. He was an expert at maneuvering a woman to where he wanted her without ever breaking the kiss, and in no time, they were lying on the sofa, his hand just underneath her sweater, his fingers itching to remove it and her bra so he could finally hold her plump breasts.

She offered no resistance as he slipped his hand up her back and unhooked her bra, and she moaned when he slid his fingers underneath it. Her nipple was a taut peak that he circled with his thumb, drawing a moan from her that made him even harder.

He got rid of the sweater and the bra and then pulled his own shirt up and off. She lowered her head and kissed his chest, making him close his eyes and reach for the zipper on her jeans. A few moments later, only her panties and his shorts remained. He watched her face as he dipped a finger inside her panties.

"Are you sure?" He had to ask again.

She nodded breathlessly and took him by surprise when she slid her hand inside his shorts and closed her fingers around him. "I'm sure." She stroked the length of him. "I want you; I want this."

He wanted to go slowly to make sure she was okay, but she was pumping her hand up and down now, making him close his eyes and relax into it; it felt so good. But no. He moved his hips to the side, freeing himself from her grasp, and pushed her panties down.

He slid to the floor and kneeled there to get rid of the panties, then held her knees apart and kissed her thighs. Her fingers tangled in his hair as he worked his way up. Her muscles trembled under his fingers when he finally trailed his tongue over her opening. She was already soaking for him.

"Logan!" she breathed.

He reluctantly lifted his head. "You want me to stop?"

She shook her head rapidly. "Don't you dare!"

He chuckled and dipped his head again. He slid a finger inside and felt her tense, her muscles clenching him tight, making him realize he wouldn't be able to hold out for long. He needed to feel her do that around his cock, not just his finger.

He needn't have worried about this taking too long. She began to rock her hips and let out low moans. "Oh, Logan, that feels so good."

He moved his hand and his tongue in time with her, not sure who picked up the pace, but knowing for sure as she gripped his finger and his hair tighter and tighter, that she was close.

"Oh, oh, oh! Logan! Yes!"

He thrust his finger deeper and deeper as he felt her come, lapping her with his tongue and taking her taut clit in his mouth to suck harder and harder until she finally stilled.

"Oh, wow!"

He looked up at her, and the sight of her flushed face above her heaving breasts deterred him from giving her the breather that he'd planned to. He got rid of his shorts and sat on the sofa beside her, pulling her into his arms to kiss her, then fondling her amazing breasts as he drew her on top of him, straddling his lap.

She gasped as his cock jerked against her. He gasped too, flooded with need as he pushed into her wetness.

She put her hands on his shoulders and held his gaze as he moved his hand between them, touching her, opening her up to receive him.

He cupped her breast and took her hard nipple into his mouth, closing his eyes as she wrapped her fingers around him and guided him into her. She was moving so slowly, driving him crazy, and then she thrust her hips, impaling herself on him. She was so hot and so tight that he cried out her name as he pushed deep inside.

That seemed to ignite her, and instead of the slow, gentle start he'd planned to restrain himself, he thrust deep and hard, rising up to penetrate deeper and deeper and in rhythm with her wild ride. She grasped the back of the sofa above his shoulders and let her head fall back, moaning as she took him. He held onto her hips to pull her down deeper and mouthed her breasts, making her scream. The tension was building at the base of his spine, sending out ripples of building pleasure each time he thrust inside her. He wasn't going to last long, but she was already ahead of him. She started to tighten around him and move faster still, encouraging him to let go. He reached his climax deep inside her, and she screamed again as she joined him, their bodies moving together in a frantic coupling that made him tingle from his toes to his scalp as he came. He saw stars behind his eyes as the pleasure crashed through him and into her, and then washed back over him again and again.

Eventually, she slumped down with her head against his shoulder, breathing hard.

"Oh, my God! What did you do to me?"

He nibbled the side of her neck, making her body quiver and sending aftershocks through him.

"I just gave you a little preview of things to come."

She lifted her head and looked down into his eyes. "A little preview?" she asked incredulously.

He grinned. "That's right. We're just getting started, babe."

"I don't know about started. I think you just finished me off."

He chuckled. "For now, maybe."

She dropped a kiss on his lips, and he realized it was the first time she'd kissed him without waiting for him. "I like the sound of that."

He ran his thumb over her nipple and loved the way it stiffened in response. "Good, because you're going to get used to this if it's up to me."

She smiled. "I'll happily get used to it." Her smile faded. "Hopefully, I'll get better at it, too."

He frowned. "Better? You can't beat perfection, and if you're telling me that wasn't perfect …"

She made a face and rolled off him. "I know you're used to women with a lot more experience than I have."

"Don't, Rox. They were just fun. That was just sex. It didn't mean anything. With you … this … it's different. Better. So much better. It's more than just physical. It means a lot."

She searched his face for a moment and then nodded and got to her feet and picked up her clothes. "I hope so. I'll be back in a minute."

He frowned as she disappeared into the powder room in the hallway. He supposed he couldn't blame her for being wary of him and questioning his intentions, but he needed her to know; this was real for him.

Roxy couldn't help smiling at herself in the mirror in the bathroom while she cleaned up and got dressed. It had been a long time since she'd had sex—and she didn't think she'd ever had sex as good as that. He was amazing! She'd assumed that he would be—he'd had enough practice. She frowned as she zipped up her jeans. She needed to stop thinking like that— stop thinking about the fact that he'd been with so many women. It didn't make her feel good—about him or about herself. She needed to learn to trust what he said about this being different, about her being different. She wanted to, but like he'd said himself, it would take time. Her smile was back at the thought that if he wanted to prove it to her over and over and over again, he wouldn't get any complaints from her.

When she came out of the bathroom, he was coming back down the stairs. He came to her and closed his arms around her. "Are you okay?"

She reached up and landed a peck on his lips. "More than okay. Sorry I ran to hide in the bathroom like that."

His smile was so gentle. It was a side to him she hadn't seen before. He was being encouraging, supportive, and she liked it. "It's okay. I get it. As long as it was only for a minute and you're over it now?"

"I am. It just felt weird." She laughed. "Don't look like that. It felt great while we were doing it, but now we've crossed that line, and I didn't know how to be."

"Do you need to be any different than you were before?"

"No. I figured that out while I was in the bathroom."

"Good. I don't want you to be weirded out. I don't want things to change between us. Well, that's not true. I do want things to change, to get better. What I don't want is for you to pull away from me."

"I won't. I'm going to trust you and see where this goes. So, don't let me down."

He shook his head solemnly. "I won't. I promise. I might get some things wrong, but it won't be on purpose, and I'll fix them as soon as I can."

She smiled. "It's not all pressure on you, you know. I don't see this as you having to prove something to me. I see it as us trying to work it out together."

He smiled back at her. "Like a team? I like that idea."

"Me too, but before we can become a team, we each need to figure out how the other works, then we can work together."

"Yep. You're right. What do you say, do you want to stay the night?"

Her heart raced in her chest. She hadn't been expecting that. She shook her head slowly. "I don't think so. I'm at work in the morning. So are you. I don't want ..." She didn't know what she wanted to say, all she knew was that she wasn't ready to spend the night with him.

He gave her a rueful smile. "So, you're going to screw my brains out and then leave me to sleep alone?"

"Yeah, I guess I am."

"Maybe next weekend?"

"Maybe."

"But it's not time for you to go yet anyway. Come on, let's hang out for a while longer."

She followed him back into the living room. She didn't want to leave yet, that wouldn't feel right either.

~ ~ ~

It was just after ten when Logan pulled his truck up outside her house. "Thanks for today, Rox."

"Thank you. I had a good time."

"When can I see you again?"

She shrugged. "When do you want to?"

"Tomorrow." He grinned. He didn't see any point in beating about the bush. He wanted to see her tomorrow and the next night and the next.

"Okay. I won't be home from work till about seven-thirty, though."

"Do you want to come to my place when you're done? I can make us dinner."

She raised an eyebrow at him. "You cook?"

He grinned. "I'm a man of many talents. I cook, I clean, I keep house pretty well if I do say so myself."

She laughed. "You do it all yourself? I have to tell you, your place is so nice I assumed you had a cleaner."

He laughed. "I told you that you should never assume. I like housework, it keeps my hands busy while my brain shuts down."

"Well, if ever you need any more downtime for your brain, my house could use some help."

He smirked. "If you're serious, I'd be happy to help." He winked. "I didn't like to say anything."

She slapped his arm. "Are you saying my house needs cleaning?"

He pressed his lips together and shook his head. "Na-ah. No way would I say such a thing."

She laughed. "You just think it. And you're right, of course. I'd never dream of asking you to do it, though. But you've pricked my conscience enough that I'll get onto it on my next day off."

"If you let me be your cleaner, then you could spend your days off doing more fun things with me."

He loved the way her eyes sparkled. "Hmm, you might be able to persuade me with that."

They both looked up as a car turned into the street, and headlights illuminated the cab of the truck.

"I should go in."

"Yeah. I'll see you tomorrow. Just come over to my place whenever you get done at work."

"Okay, but I'll text when I'm on the way."

He leaned across the console and cupped her cheek in his hand. "Goodnight, Rox." He brushed his lips over hers, wishing that he was going inside with her, or that she'd stayed at his place. He wanted to know how it felt to sleep beside her, to wake up next to her.

When she eventually broke the kiss, she gave him a look he didn't understand. "Goodnight."

He watched her walk up the path to her front door and then turn and wave. He waited until she was safely inside before he pulled away.

It was only a short drive back to his place. Normally, he would have walked her home, but it was so cold. He thought for a minute about turning the truck toward town and going to see if anyone was at the Boathouse, but he decided against it. If he saw any of the guys, they'd want to know how he'd spent the day, and as much as he might want to brag, there was no way he'd tell anyone what he and Roxy had been up to. It'd be up to her to share that, if and when she chose to.

He pulled back into his driveway a few minutes later and pulled his phone out of his pocket when it beeped with a text. He was hoping it'd be Roxy saying goodnight. He blew out a sigh when he saw the message. It was a girl who lived in San Francisco and came up here a couple of times a year—wanting to know if he'd be around next weekend. He planned to make sure that he wasn't!

Chapter Twelve

"Well?" asked Angel the minute Roxy walked into the office on Monday morning.

Roxy grinned. "Well, what? And by the way, good morning, and I hope you had a good weekend."

Angel made a face. "Don't give me that. I want to know what happened after you left on Saturday night."

"Logan walked me home."

"And?"

Roxy tried to hide her smile, but she couldn't manage it.

"See! That smile says it all. Except it doesn't say enough. Did he spend the night?"

"No! You know I like him, but you also know what I think about one-night stands. There's no way I would have done that." She wasn't about to admit how close she'd been to inviting Logan to come in with her on Saturday night—or Friday night, for that matter.

"Sorry." Angel looked put out. "I just thought something was finally going to happen between the two of you. I mean, he made no secret of the fact that he wanted it to."

"Something is happening. I just didn't want to start out by becoming yet another notch on his bedpost."

"Grr. So, tell me what *is* happening. I want to be excited for you."

"Sorry." Roxy grinned. "We spent the day together yesterday, and he asked me to be his girlfriend."

"Oh, wow! His girlfriend?"

"Yeah. It took me by surprise, too. But I like it. I said, yes."

"Oh, Roxy, that's awesome. Although …"

"It's okay. I know you're probably as concerned as I am. He's not exactly boyfriend material, is he?"

"He hasn't been. Up to this point. But that doesn't mean he can't be going forward. Even guys who like to play the field meet a girl who's worth giving it all up for at some point. They change. Maybe you're that girl for Logan."

"Maybe." Roxy didn't know what to say to that because she didn't know what to think. Of course, she'd wondered if things might turn out that way for Logan and her, but she didn't want to set herself up for a big disappointment—and she didn't want him to feel that she was trying to tie him down. "All I need to know for now is that we're seeing each other, and it's good."

Angel raised an eyebrow at her. "And at some point soon, you'll get to find out how good *being* with Logan really is."

Roxy felt her cheeks flush but didn't answer.

"Oh, my God! You already know, don't you?! I thought you said he didn't stay over on Saturday night?"

"He didn't."

"But you spent the day in bed with him yesterday?"

"No. We watched the game, and we went for a walk on the beach ... and we may have spent part of the evening on the sofa."

Angel grinned. "Good for you! Well, was it ... good for you?"

Roxy nodded happily. "I'd always had this idea that he must be pretty great. I mean—he's had enough practice, but Angel ..." She was embarrassed, but she didn't mind telling her friend just how great it had been. "He's amazing!"

Angel clapped her hands together. "That's awesome, Roxy. Oh, I hope this works out. It'd be so nice if the two of you get together for real."

Roxy nodded. She didn't want to let herself think too much about that possibility. "It's way too early to think about that just yet."

Angel gave her a knowing smile. "If you say so."

They both looked up at the sound of a tap on the office door. "Good morning, ladies." Ben, who owned the Lodge, came in and smiled at them. Are we ready for the Monday morning meeting, or do we need coffee first?"

Roxy grinned at him. "I need coffee. Do you want me to get you one? Angel's no doubt had three cups already."

"Please, Roxy," said Ben.

Angel shrugged. "You know me too well. We'll meet you in the conference room."

When Roxy got to the conference room, the way the two of them smiled at her made her suspicious.

"What's going on?" she asked as she set Ben's coffee down in front of him.

"We're scheming," he replied with a smile. "I know your talents are under-utilized in your current role, and I was wondering if you'd like to take on more responsibility."

Roxy looked at him and then at Angel and back again. "What kind of responsibility?"

"Don't worry," said Angel. "You won't be treading on my toes if that's what you're thinking."

It was exactly what Roxy had been thinking, and she didn't like the idea.

"No," said Ben. "This is a new project. Jack and Pete, who own the development at Four Mile, want to trial a program that brings people up here on mini vacations; people will stay here at the Lodge for a couple of days and tour the model homes. It will give them a better idea of what it's like here and hopefully encourage them to buy vacation or second homes at the development."

Roxy nodded. She could see the logic in that. One of the hotels she'd worked at before had done something similar, but they'd sold timeshares. "It sounds like a good idea, but where do I come in?"

Ben grinned. "I need someone to coordinate the vacation promotion. I know you've done that kind of thing before. And … we need a point of contact with the team on-site over there, to keep up with which properties are available to tour and the schedule of which will be available for sale and when."

She nodded and looked at Angel, who was grinning at her.

Ben raised an eyebrow. "Are you in?"

"I might be if you want to tell me why you're both grinning like idiots."

"You're a bit slow sometimes, Roxy," said Angel.

"About what?"

"You haven't asked who you'd be working with on-site."

"Oh!" It made sense. Logan was the one in charge of the build schedule. He would be the one who said which properties could be toured and which ones would be available for sale next. She shot an evil look at Angel. She might have expected such meddling from her. But Ben? How did he even know about her and Logan?

To his credit, he hung his head. "Sorry. I don't mean to interfere. And it's not a setup—not really. Jack and Pete have been kicking this idea around for a while, and I've kept saying I'd get on it. Now just seems like the ideal time. Are you interested?"

"Sure." She liked the idea of having a project all of her own to work on. She loved Angel but didn't love always being in her shadow at work. She didn't think working with Logan would be a problem. In fact, it would be a good way to get to know him better—outside of the bedroom.

"Great," said Ben. "I'll email you everything I've pulled together so far, and we can talk about it when I'm over here on Wednesday, then we can set up a meeting with Logan early next week."

"Great."

The meeting moved on to all the usual Monday morning business, but Roxy's mind kept straying back to this new project. She hoped Logan would like the idea of them working together—and that they'd get along well.

~ ~ ~

Logan stopped and looked around when he heard someone calling his name in the grocery store. He hoped whoever it was didn't want to keep him for long. He'd only come to get some flowers for Roxy. He stepped away from them when he saw Ivan hurrying toward him.

"Hey. How's it going?"

"I'm doing great. How about you? Are you all settled in?"

"I am. It's weird being here pretty much full time, but I like it."

"It's a good place. Are you finding your feet okay?" Logan felt a little guilty. Ivan hadn't lived here for long, and the two of them had hung out a few times when he first arrived. Logan had said he'd be around for him if he needed anything but hadn't made the effort to check in with him lately.

Ivan grinned. "I'm fine. I'm perfectly capable of doing for myself. I don't need help; I wouldn't mind some company, though. It seems like most folks here are coupled up. Do you want to go for a beer at the weekend?"

Logan's heart sank. He'd offered to do just that, any time Ivan wanted to. At the time, he'd rather have done that than spend an evening in the company of yet another woman. Now, things were different. He wanted to spend his time with

Roxy—and he didn't like the idea of telling her that he couldn't see her because he was going out with his buddy.

Ivan raised an eyebrow. "That face says you already have other plans."

Logan nodded. "I just started seeing someone. I don't know what we're doing yet, but I hope we're doing something."

"That's okay. I wouldn't want to impose. I just thought you were in the same boat I am."

"I always have been, up until now. I feel bad."

"Don't. I'd trade places with you. I'd rather go out with a girl than with you. It's just not an option for me."

"Of course, it is. I'll bet there are plenty of girls who'd love to go out with you."

Ivan laughed. "Yeah, there probably are. I didn't mean poor sad me. I just meant I don't know anyone yet, and I'm not like you. I couldn't just walk up to a woman I don't know and end up going home with her at the end of the night."

Logan made a face. That was exactly how he'd been for as long as he could remember, but it didn't sound too good when he heard someone else describe him that way. "Then you should get to know everyone. The gang usually all goes out together at least one night over the weekend. How about I give you a call when I know what's happening. You should come, get to know everyone better—the girls and the guys. Then you'll have more options for dates and for buddies."

"Thanks. I'd like that." Ivan eyed the flowers. "Are you buying some?"

Logan nodded guiltily.

"Don't look guilty about it. I think it's great. Who is she? I'm thinking she has to be someone special if she's got you turned around so quickly. What was it, love at first sight or something?"

Logan grinned. "Not exactly. I've known her for a few years. I've always liked her, but I only thought of her as a friend, not as a woman." He blew out a sigh. "That sounds stupid now, even to me. It's just that I only thought of women one way. And I would never have dared think about Roxy like that. She was always telling me I was a pig the way I treated women."

"Roxy? Damn! I can see why you like her. She's a good-looking woman. But I'm surprised at you. I thought you'd have gone for someone a little more …"

"What?" Logan wondered what he was about to say.

"I don't know, someone meeker, more amenable if that's the right word. Roxy strikes me as someone you just don't mess with. She's strong, smart." Ivan grinned. "I like her."

"Yeah, she's all of that and more. That's why I like her. And I might be taking on more than I can handle. I feel like I have a lot to live up to if I'm going to be …worthy of her." He looked at Ivan. "That's a weird thing to say, isn't it?"

"Nope. I think it's an awesome thing to say. And it makes it sound like you're ready to step up. The Logan I thought I knew wouldn't have given a crap about being worthy of a woman."

"You're right. That's who I've been, but apparently, I'm changing." He grinned. "And I like it." He checked his watch. "In fact, she's on her way to my place after work, so I'm going to get these and get my ass home. I'll call you about coming out at the weekend. And I'll introduce you to the guys from work, too. Most of them are still single and are up for going out for a beer pretty much any time you might want to."

"Thanks," said Ivan. "I appreciate it."

"Sure thing."

Logan grinned to himself as he took a bunch of red roses to the self-checkout. As he'd watched Luke and Zack meet Angel and Maria and fall in love with them, he'd thought that they were crazy for taking themselves off the market so quickly. As he'd seen their relationships develop, he could admit that a tiny part of him had envied them. Now, he realized, he was eager to follow in their footsteps, and he was hoping that he and Roxy might be able to turn their friendship into something more.

~ ~ ~

On Wednesday evening, Roxy pulled her car to a stop in Logan's driveway, just as she'd done every night this week. She was enjoying the way things were working out between them.

The front door opened as she got out of the car, and he stood there in the warm light from the hallway and held his arms out to her. She trotted up the steps and leaned against him.

"Hey, honey. You're home," he said with a grin.

Her heart thudded to a halt. She knew he was only making a play on the words, but still. It pulled her up short. The thought of this being home—of him being the person she shared a home with? She drew in a deep breath and let it out slowly. That was silly, and she knew it.

She made herself smile as she looked up at him and played along. "Did you have a nice day at the office, dear?"

He nodded and dropped a kiss on her lips. Something in his eyes told her that he'd had the same feeling that she did. Though he didn't acknowledge it. Poor guy. If it had freaked her out, it must have been ten times worse for him. "I did. I missed you, though."

She laughed. "You haven't had time to miss me. I said goodnight to you right here less than …" She looked at her watch. She'd left here at just after eleven last night, and it was now almost seven. "Twenty hours ago."

He nodded. "But that's such a long time. You know, if you'd stayed with me, it would only have been twelve hours ago. In fact, we could have ridden to work together—and back, and that would make it more like eleven."

She laughed. "Exactly. I reckon you're going to tire of me sooner or later. And I'd rather the time that we spend together before you do is quality time."

His eyes widened, and he tightened his arms around her. "I'm never going to tire of you; are you crazy?"

Her heart raced. He couldn't really mean that, could he? He smirked and let go of her, taking her hand to lead her into the house. "It's okay. You don't need to answer that. I know you must be crazy to go out with me in the first place. Forget I asked."

She followed him inside and let it go, but she didn't think she'd be able to forget about what he'd said. That he'd never tire of her? She liked that idea a whole lot more than she should, but she couldn't allow herself to believe it. She had to enjoy what they had while it lasted—and be realistic about the fact that it probably wouldn't last too long. She believed that he was sincere in his interest in her. They were having a lot of fun—and great sex. But she didn't believe that a guy like him would be happy being tied to just one woman for the long term. He might want to. She believed him when he said that he did. But he'd get bored, restless. There were so many beautiful women that came up here, attractive women who considered sleeping with a sexy local to be the highlight of their vacation. He might stick with her through the winter, but she fully expected that by the time the summer season rolled around, he'd be back to his old ways—if not before.

Chapter Thirteen

Logan looked himself over in the mirror and smiled. He looked good, even if he did say so himself. He usually made an effort on a Friday night, but tonight was especially important. It was the first time that he and Roxy were going out with their friends as an official couple. He was also hoping that it would be the first time that she spent the night with him. They'd spent every evening together this last week, but she hadn't wanted to stay over. He'd gone over to her place last night, but she'd shooed him out of there just after eleven. It wasn't like they weren't spending any time in bed—and he was loving that. A wave of desire rushed through him at the thought of it—but he wanted to sleep with her in the more literal sense. There was something about it that felt important to him.

He picked his phone up off the counter when it rang.

"Hey, Colt. What's up?"

"Hey. I just wanted to check if you're coming out tonight."

"Of course, I am. It's Friday, isn't it?"

"Yeah, but I didn't know if you and Roxy would have other plans."

"Nope. We'll be there."

"So, the two of you are officially a *we* now, then?"

"That's right. And I have to tell you. I'm liking it."

"Good for you."

"You should try it. Find yourself a nice girl and couple up."

Colt laughed. "I would if I could find a nice girl. I've been open to the idea for a long time. But between my job and my apparent inability to attract a nice girl, it hasn't happened for me."

"Aww. We should find you someone. What about Amber or Jade?"

Colt laughed. "No, thanks. They're nice girls, but I don't see them that way. Even if I did, I think Austin has his eye on Amber, and Jade's too scary."

Logan laughed with him. "Yeah, she's not exactly meek and mild. She's feisty. She's good people, though."

"Oh, they both are, but I'm not interested in either of them that way."

"Well, I'm not the best one to help you find a girl, but I can steer you toward another single guy who's new in town and looking for buddies. Maybe the two of you can hunt together, be each other's wingman."

"I don't need a wingman. I'm not even looking really. I'm just kind of in shock that you're settling down before me."

"I think everyone is—especially me."

"Who are you talking about, anyway? Who's the new arrival?"

"Well, he's been here a little while now, but he's not been venturing out much. You know Ivan?"

"He's the guy who works for Seymour Davenport, right?"

"That's him."

"Yeah. I've run into him a couple of times. Seems like a good guy."

"He is. He's coming out tonight."

"Cool. I'll buy him a beer."

"And maybe introduce him to some of the local ladies?"

"I may as well. I know everyone in town, and there's no one here for me. Maybe Ivan will have better luck."

Logan frowned. "You make it sound like you wish there was someone here for you."

"Ignore me. I'm happy the way I am. I wouldn't have time for a girl anyway. The job makes sure of that. I suppose I'm just a little bit envious of you and Roxy. I hope it works for you. Maybe part of it is that I can see our group of single friends dwindling. The group of couples is getting bigger, and I know we're all still buddies, but hanging with couples isn't the same … Like I said, just ignore me. I don't mean anything by it."

"I know what you mean."

"Yeah. It's just part of life. We're at that age where things change." He laughed. "Next step is that you'll all start having babies. I won't be envious about that, though."

"Yeah." Logan couldn't help but smile. He loved kids. With three older sisters, he had lots of nieces and nephews, and he loved them all. The idea of having kids of his own someday made him happy. But it wasn't anything he needed to get excited about just yet. First, he had to get the hang of being in a real relationship.

"I'll see you in a while, then."

"Okay. Is everyone else coming?"

"As far as I know. I talked to Austin this morning, and he said he is."

"Okay. I'll see you there."

When they arrived at the Boathouse, Logan slung his arm around Roxy's shoulders and smiled at her.

She smiled back. "Is this weird for you?"

"No. Different. But good different, not weird different. How about you?"

"If I'm honest, it is weird. I've been coming out by myself ever since I came to live here. I mean, it's nice to be part of a couple. But …" she hesitated, not sure what he'd think if she told him the truth, but she had to be honest. "You're not someone I expected to see as part of a couple, let alone to be with."

"I know." He dropped a kiss on her lips. "Don't look so worried. I'm not offended. How could I be? I get it. I'm just happy that I'm getting to prove you wrong. I won't let you down, Rox."

"I know you don't plan to, but I want you to promise me that when you've had enough, when you get bored of this and want to go back to … being you, you'll just tell me. No hard feelings."

He tightened his arm around her. "Thanks. But I don't see that happening."

She pressed her lips together. She liked the idea that it might not happen, but what would that mean? If he never got tired of being part of a couple with her, then they wouldn't break up. She searched his face. He was serious; he wasn't joking or bullshitting her, she could tell.

"Hey, guys." She turned to Austin, coming in just behind them. He made a point of eyeing Logan's arm around her shoulders, then raised an eyebrow. "It's true then? You two are together?"

Logan grinned. "We are. For as long as she'll have me."

Austin laughed and looked at Roxy. "What have you done to him?"

"I have no idea. I'm as surprised as you are."

"Well, good luck to you both."

"Thanks, but I'm already feeling lucky enough," said Logan. "Shall we go join the others?"

They made their way over to a big table where Angel and Luke and Maria and Zack were sitting with Colt, Amber, and Jade.

Maria greeted them with a smile. "Hi. You're just in time. Are you guys free the weekend after next?"

"I can be," said Austin. "Why? What's happening?"

"We're talking about renting a cabin in the mountains. With all this cold weather, they've had early snow. I haven't seen snow in years. And we're thinking it'd be a fun weekend away as a group." She caught Roxy's eye. "What do you say? Do you two want to come?"

Roxy looked at Angel. "I don't know. I'd have to see what the schedule is at work." It was safer to voice her doubt about being able to get the time off than to say she wasn't sure about how she and Logan would stand on it.

Angel grinned at her. "I already checked with Ben. He doesn't mind being on call for Kallen if we both want to go."

Logan grinned at her. "Great. We can go then, right."

Roxy nodded, surprised at his enthusiasm. "It looks like it."

"Who all's going then?" asked Austin.

"Us," said Maria, nodding at Zack. "Angel and Luke. Colt if can get the whole weekend off."

"And us," added Jade. "Grandma's almost back to normal now. She practically begged us to go when I mentioned it. I think she's getting sick of us still trying to babysit her."

Amber laughed. "She is. And I can't say I blame her. She's been so independent for so many years. She appreciated our help after her heart attack, but she wants to get back to normal now. I think she hopes that sending us away for the weekend will somehow prove to us that she doesn't need us anymore."

"Does that mean the two of you don't plan to stay here?" asked Austin.

Roxy tried to hide a smile. She knew that he would hate the idea of them moving away—especially Amber.

Jade shrugged. "I don't know." She looked at her sister. "We're going to have to talk about that at some point."

Amber nodded but didn't say anything. Roxy didn't know her too well, but she'd guess that she wasn't any more eager to leave than Austin was to see her go.

"How would you guys feel about asking Ivan?" asked Logan.

Roxy looked up at him.

"I ran into him earlier in the week. I think he's at a bit of a loose end. It'd be good for him to get to know more people. He might be coming tonight, too."

Jade waggled her eyebrows. "I wouldn't have any complaints."

Amber gave her a stern look but didn't say anything.

"Really?" asked Logan. "I should introduce the two of you properly."

Angel laughed. "What's with you? Now that you're with Roxy, you think you can start fixing other people up, too?"

Logan grinned at her. "Why not? Now that I know how good being in a relationship is, I want everyone to know the joy."

The others laughed. Roxy did, too, but part of her had to wonder if he was just joking—surely, he didn't mean that. They'd only been seeing each other a week.

"No matter how good your intentions might be," said Angel, "you still have a lot to learn when it comes to being a matchmaker. It's not Jade you should be introducing Ivan to." She smiled at Jade. "You're only interested in looking, right?"

Jade nodded. "Yeah. He's eye candy, that's all. I'm not interested."

Roxy wondered what Jade's story was. She was beautiful. She turned heads everywhere she went, but she was prickly toward guys, toward most people, really.

Logan shrugged. "Yeah. I'm not an expert."

"It sounds like you are, though." Luke looked at Angel. "The way you said it's not Jade he should introduce Ivan to, made it sound like there's someone else."

Angel smirked. "Maybe there is, but it's not my place to say."

Roxy had an idea she knew who Angel was talking about.

"Why not invite her to come away—whoever she is?" asked Logan.

Maria shook her head. "It's a big cabin, but it's not that big. It has five bedrooms. I reckon three couples, and then the singles can figure out how to share the other two rooms. I wouldn't want anyone to have to share with people they don't know."

The conversation moved on, as they talked about who could go and how they'd get there. But Roxy was caught up in thinking about how quickly and easily Maria was including her and Logan as one of the couples. She liked the idea, but it felt a little bit like tempting fate. She'd rather take things slowly. If they were going to get serious, then it made sense to build a solid foundation. And if Logan was going to get bored, as she assumed he would, she'd rather not have rushed in too deep before it ended.

~ ~ ~

Roxy was quiet as they walked home. She'd been quieter than usual for most of the evening.

Logan took hold of her hand and tugged on it. "Want to tell me what's wrong?"

She smiled. "Nothing, why?"

"I get the feeling that you're noodling something through in that brain of yours." He tapped on the side of her head. "Is everything okay? Did I do something wrong tonight?"

"No! You didn't do anything wrong at all. I enjoyed it. I enjoyed your company."

"But?"

"There really isn't a but."

He frowned. "Would you tell me if there was?"

She smiled. "Probably."

"Why do I get the feeling that that's a probably leaning toward no?"

She sighed. "Because that's likely the truth."

He was starting to feel edgy. He'd thought that it was a great evening—that they'd enjoyed it together. Now he felt like he was missing something. "Come on, Rox. You made me promise you that I'd be honest with you about how I feel. Can't you do the same?"

"Yeah. I should. I'm sorry. Aren't you worried that this is going a little too fast?"

He frowned. "No! Are you?"

She shrugged, and his heart sank. "What are you saying?"

"That maybe you don't need the pressure of people assuming that we're one of the couples now. I mean, we've only been seeing each other a week."

"It doesn't feel like pressure to me. It feels like acceptance. If I'm honest. When Maria said that, it felt like the rest of them had known for a long time that we'd be one of the couples, and it was just me who was slow to realize it."

"You weren't the only one."

"Are you saying you don't want it to be that way?"

"No. Honestly, Logan, I'm not. I like the idea. But I know what you're like. I don't want this to feel like you're getting locked into something with me. I don't want it to be too hard for you to get out of when you've had enough."

He stopped walking and put his hands on her shoulders. "You don't have any faith in me, do you?"

"It's not like that. I do have faith in you. I know you're being as straightforward with me as you can be, and I appreciate it. But I know who you are, and this isn't you. I want to make the most of it while it lasts, but I don't want you to feel trapped."

He frowned. "I don't. I feel happy and excited about what the future might hold for us. I feel hopeful—or at least I did. Now you're making me wonder if I'm just kidding myself. Are you saying that this doesn't mean anything to you? That you don't want to be tied down to me?"

She laughed. "No. All I'm doing is trying to be realistic about the fact that it probably won't happen."

"Because you don't want it to?"

"Because I don't think you will."

"So, you don't believe anything I say?" He tried not to sound hurt.

She blew out a sigh. "I'm not saying I don't trust you. I guess if anything, I don't trust myself. I'm trying not to let myself feel too excited or too hopeful—because I'm preparing myself for when you don't want to keep seeing me."

He closed his arms around her and hugged her tight to his chest. "I'm sorry I make you feel that way. I'm doing my best here."

She buried her face in his chest. "And you're doing great. You're doing everything you can. You couldn't do anything more. It's my fault. I'm judging you on how you were, not how you're being with me. I know it's not fair, but I have years of evidence that says you only see women one way. I only have a week's experience with this new you. I like it. I want it to last, but can you see what I mean?"

He nodded sadly. "Of course, I can, Rox. I'm surprised at myself that I feel the way I do about you. That I've changed so much, so fast. I know in my heart that I'm not going to change back. This is it. You're it for me. You're what I want. But just because I know it doesn't mean that you can. It'll take time for me to convince you—to prove to you. And I'm prepared to do that. I want to ask you not to doubt me, but that wouldn't be fair. You have every right to, but can I ask you to at least let me keep showing you?"

"Yes."

"Thanks."

They started walking again, and instead of taking her home, he turned when he came to his street.

She looked up at him. "It's late."

"It is, and it's probably too late if you think that I'm going to take you to my place to have my wicked way with you and then walk you home afterward."

She laughed. "I know. I thought you were coming to my place."

"I can if that's what you want. But what I'd really like is for you to come with me and stay the night."

He watched the struggle on her face. She'd made excuses all week about why they couldn't spend the whole night together. He was prepared to hear another one, but this felt like a make or break moment. She didn't fully trust that he wanted her to be more than just a friend he went out with and slept with. He wanted her to understand that he was inviting her into his life, not just his bed.

"You're not working tomorrow. Neither am I." He winked at her. "I'll go to the bakery early and bring you back breakfast in bed."

She smiled. "That's bribery."

"I know. I'm not above bribery or any other kind of persuasion I can think of."

Her face relaxed. "I can think of a couple of ways you could persuade me."

"Oh, yeah?"

She nodded.

"Are you going to tell me what they are?"

She shook her head.

"But, I need to get you into bed to figure out what they are?"

She chuckled. "Yep."

"Okay." For a moment, he wondered if she was more interested in the sex than in spending the night together to bring them closer. He shook his head. It was a crazy thought, but it gave him a little insight into how it might be for her.

Chapter Fourteen

On Sunday afternoon, they watched football on the TV again. It was too cold outside to do much of anything, and if Roxy was honest, she didn't want to go out, anyway.

She'd only been home for clothes and toiletries since she came back to Logan's place with him on Friday night, and part of her didn't want to go even now. She loved his place. It was warm and welcoming, cozy.

He nudged her in the ribs with his elbow from his seat on the sofa beside her. "Whatcha thinkin'? Do I need to worry?"

"About what?"

He leaned closer and curled his arm around her. "I'm guessing that you're thinking about going home and getting ready for work tomorrow, and I don't want you to go."

She rested her head against his shoulder. "You're half right. I was thinking about needing to do that, but I don't want to go." She looked up at the clock on the wall. "We don't need to think about it yet; it's early."

He brushed her hair away from her face and planted a kiss on her forehead. "I've been thinking about it for a while."

Her heart hammered in her chest. Was he waiting for her to leave? She started to get to her feet. "I'm sorry. You should have said!"

He caught hold of her arm and pulled her back down beside him. "I wish you'd start to believe me, just a little bit. I'm not saying I want you to go. I'm saying ..." He hesitated, and his eyebrows drew together. "What the hell, I'm going to say it. You're trying not to put any pressure on me, so I've been trying not to put any on you. I apologize in advance if this feels like pressure, but I don't want you to go. I want you to stay. I want to wake up with you in the morning and get ready for work together. I want to see how we do with being part of each other's lives, not just playing at it on the weekends."

She held his gaze for a long moment. Her heart was racing even faster now.

"Don't ask me if I'm serious. You should know that I wouldn't dream of saying that if I wasn't."

She nodded slowly.

"And before you shoot me down, tell me why we shouldn't give it a try?"

She swallowed. The only reason she could think of was because she didn't want to put pressure on him—didn't want to cage him in a situation he didn't want to be in.

He watched her face. "And don't give me any bullshit about wanting to do what's right for me. Tell me what you want for yourself."

Eventually, she smiled. "What do I want for myself? I'd love to stay here. I'd love to get ready for work with you in the mornings and see how we go. I keep saying that I don't want to put pressure on you—the truth is that I don't want to commit to this if I'm only going to end up getting hurt when you change your mind."

"And I'm not going to change my mind. I want this, Rox. I want you. I want us."

Her heart felt like it might explode in her chest when he said that. She knew he meant it. The truth of it shone in his eyes as he looked into hers. "What do you say, should we go over to your place and get whatever you're going to need for the week?"

"The whole week?"

"Yeah. I wanted to say the month, but I didn't think you'd go for that. So, let's start with a week."

She nodded. A week was no big deal. It was long enough for them to get the idea of whether they'd get along and have fun, but not so long that it felt like a major commitment. They were just testing the water. "Okay. Let's do it."

Logan pulled the truck to a stop in front of the Lodge at seven-ten on Tuesday morning. He leaned across the console and kissed her. "Do you want to meet me for lunch?"

Roxy made a face.

"What does that look mean? Are you trying to say that you see enough of me as it is?"

She laughed. "No. I'm trying to say that you've forgotten that we'll see each other before lunchtime."

"We will?"

"Unless you forget the meeting. And I'll warn you, if you do, you'll be in deep doo-doo, Mr. Perkins. I might let you get away with a lot of things, but when it comes to work, I expect you to be professional."

He chuckled. "I hadn't forgotten." He pulled her closer and slid his hand inside her blouse. "But are you saying I won't be able to do this in our meeting?"

He cupped her breast and teased her nipple through the lacy fabric. He loved the way she sagged against him and the little noises she made in his ear.

"You're a bad, bad man Logan Perkins," she breathed.

"But you love me."

She sat up straight with a look of panic on her face. He felt it, too. Why in hell had he said that? It was just a turn of phrase. It didn't mean anything. He smiled in an attempt to let the moment slide by without making a big deal out of it. His hand was still inside her shirt, and he circled his thumb over the little hard peak that strained under his touch. "You love it. I can tell."

She nodded and closed her eyes for a moment, though whether it was to enjoy his hand on her or to get past what he'd just said, he wasn't sure.

When she opened them, she nodded. "I do. You could persuade me of most things while you're doing that. Which is why—to answer your question—no, you won't be able to do that in our meeting. That or anything like it. Do you understand me?"

He hung his head. "I can't touch you or kiss you? You're not going let me peel your clothes off and take you on the conference room table?"

She laughed, and the sound of it dispelled the last of the tension between them. "I like the sound of that. But if we're going do it, we'll have to sneak over here on our own time and do it. There's no way you're making it part of our meeting. You'd walk out of there with everything you want, and I'd be left out in the cold."

He drew her closer and hugged her as best as he could over the console. "I might take you up on the offer to sneak into the conference room sometime. But I need you to know if I get everything I want, you'll never be out in the cold." He wanted to tell her that he'd keep her warm for the rest of her days if she'd let him. He didn't say it because he knew she still didn't believe in him that much. Words were cheap. Only time and actions would prove to her how serious he was.

She pulled away from him when headlights illuminated the cab. "Thanks. I'd better get in there, and you'd better get over to your office, too. I'll see you at ten."

"Okay. See you then."

~ ~ ~

"Are you still on for tonight?" Roxy looked up from her computer to see Angel standing there, leaning on the reception desk.

"Of course."

Angel smiled. "I just wanted to make sure. You and Logan seem to be inseparable these days. I wasn't sure if you'd still be on for girls' night or if he'd be picking you up and whisking you back to your little love nest at his place."

Roxy smiled. "I brought my own car today. I couldn't remember if we were having dinner here at the plaza or going back over to town to the Boathouse."

"It's the Boathouse tonight. Maria's off today, so she's not on this side of the lake. It's a trek for the others, and you and I still have to go back that way to go home anyway."

"That's true. Do you know who's coming?"

"You, me, Maria. Kenzie said she was in. I don't know about Amber and Jade. Oh, and since we're over on that side, Missy said she might come, too. I ran into her at the bakery the other morning."

"That'd be nice. I like Missy, she's awesome."

"Yeah. Kenzie said she might ask some of the other girls, too. We seem to have separated out into two groups lately, and I think that's a shame."

"Me too, but I kind of understand it. I mean, most of them are married, and a few of them have little ones. It's harder to make plans to all get together."

"It is, but it's still worth doing. I hope you'll remember that now that you and Logan are living together."

"Living together?! I wouldn't say that."

Angel looked surprised. "Oh. Sorry. I got it wrong. I thought you'd moved in with him."

"I've been staying with him this week. But that's all."

Angel smiled. "Is it? Is it just for the week, or is that what you're saying so that he doesn't freak out?"

Roxy blew out a sigh. "It's what I'm saying so that I don't freak out. Logan's all about it. It was his idea. He started out asking me to just stay for the week, but he's already talking like I'm going to be there next week."

"And you don't want to be?"

She smiled. "The way I feel right now, I do. I could get used to it. But I'm scared it'll wear off. His track record doesn't exactly inspire much confidence in a long-term future, does it?"

"I wish you'd get over that. If you ask me, I'd say that the way he's been since you got together inspires a lot of confidence. He'd done a complete one-eighty. He's nuts about you."

Roxy shook her head. "Yeah, but if it's so easy for him to change like that, why wouldn't it be easy for him to change right back? That's what I'm scared of; that he might just wake up one morning and decide that he wants his freedom back."

"He might, any one of us could do that any day. But I don't think he will, any more than I will or Luke or Zack. You need to judge him on who he is now. It seems to me that he's showing you in all kinds of ways that he's serious about you."

"He is. If I only went by what he says and does, then I'd be happy and relaxed and excited about the future."

"So why don't you do just that? You can never be one hundred percent sure that your partner isn't going to end things—no one can. But if it happens, it won't be the end of the world, you'll survive. It just makes me sad that you're not going all in. You're not even giving him a real chance."

"I am."

Angel shook her head. "Only half a chance—at best. You're the one who's living with your foot out the door and not committing."

Roxy stared at her for a long moment. She wanted to argue, but she knew that what her friend was saying was true.

Angel shrugged. "Only you can decide if he's important enough to you to give him a real shot."

"He is!"

"Then go for it."

Roxy smiled. "Thanks. I needed that kick in the butt."

"Happy to give it to you. I'd rather call you out now than have to console you when he gives up because you won't get as serious as he wants to."

"I never thought of it that way around."

"Well, if you take my advice, you'll start. Anyway, I'm leaving early, I have a couple of errands to run. I'll see you at the Boathouse at seven."

"Okay. See you then."

~ ~ ~

Logan looked around the table at his friends. "Who's still up for this weekend away?"

Zack made a face. "I really want to be; it was Maria's idea, after all. She wants to see the snow so much."

Logan raised an eyebrow. "But?"

Clay was talking about needing to go to Nashville late next week. If he does, that'll mean we're there for the weekend."

Luke nodded. "That's the trouble with our job. You can't ever make plans too far in advance because the schedule changes all the time."

Luke and Zack were pilots. The guy they flew for, Clay McAdam, was a country music singer who spent half his time here at the lake and the rest either in Nashville or traveling.

"What are you saying then? That it's off?"

Zack made a face. "I don't want to make the call just yet. It's guaranteed that if we cancel, Clay's plans will change, and we'll be able to go. I'm hanging onto the reservation. You guys can still go even if we can't."

"Maybe Maria and Angel will still want to go," added Luke.

Logan looked around at the others. "What about you?"

Colt shook his head. "I'm out. I have to work."

Austin shrugged. "I'm still up for it if anyone's going."

Logan smiled. "Does anyone mean Amber?"

Austin shook his head. "Nah. I daren't even think about asking her out."

"Why not?"

"Because Nadia's making life difficult. She's tripping me up at every chance she gets. I'm pretty sure if I started seeing someone else, she'd make trouble for them. It's just not worth it. And besides, after being in a relationship so long, it's nice to spend time on my own again. I'd forgotten what it's like." He grinned. "You and I seem to have switched roles. From what I hear, you're spending every minute of the day—and night— with Roxy. How's it going?"

Logan grinned. "It's going great. I'm hoping this trip is still going to happen. She was excited about going to the mountains and about seeing snow. Apparently, she used to be a skier, and she wants to give it a go."

Colt laughed. "Be careful if you go skiing. I'm remembering your crazy ass on the black slopes when we were kids. I'd hate for you to break your neck showing off for her."

Logan grinned. "I'm a reformed character. I'll keep it nice and sedate. Take good care of her."

"Isn't that Ivan?" asked Zack, nodding toward a guy standing at the bar by himself.

"Yeah. Do you mind if I call him over?"

"Sure. The more, the merrier."

Logan waved, and Ivan came over to join them. "Hey, guys. How's it going?"

"Great," said Logan. "We're having a catch-up while the girls are out for their weekly dinner. Want to join us?"

Ivan nodded happily. "I'd love to. It's been a long week, and up until four o'clock this afternoon, I was convinced that today was Friday. I'd promised myself a beer after work to celebrate making it to the weekend. When I finally figured out that it's only Thursday, I decided I should still come out as a consolation prize."

Austin laughed. "I get that way myself sometimes, not knowing what day it is. How's the new place? Are you settling in okay?"

"Yeah. It's great. It feels a bit strange rattling around in that big place by myself, but I like it."

"Where are you?" asked Logan.

"Down by the water near the end of Main." Ivan smiled. "I said I wanted a place by the water, and Mr. D took me at my word."

Austin laughed at the puzzled look the others gave Ivan. "To the rest of us, Mr. D is the great Seymour Davenport. He gave me strict instructions that I was only to show Ivan properties on the waterfront."

"Wow," said Colt. "And he picks up the tab, too, right? I wish I worked for a guy like that."

"He's a great guy. I've been with him a long time. He gave me a chance when no one else would have. I know I'm lucky."

"The way he talks about you, I'd say he thinks he's the lucky one," said Austin. "It must have been hard for him to walk away from his investment firm. What would he have done with himself if he didn't have you? I know he came here to be with Miss Chris, but she wouldn't stand for him resting on his laurels and doing nothing."

Ivan laughed. "Chris is awesome. I love her. She's good for him. I'm sure Mr. D would have done just fine managing all his charity work. But I'm glad he kept me on and brought me into the office to help with it."

"And before, all you did was drive him around?"

"Yeah. That, and I was kind of his security. It's not like he had any major threats coming after him." He looked at Zack. "Nothing like what I heard about you. And Clay McAdam, too. He had some issues a while back, didn't he?"

The others nodded.

"For me, it was more a case of making sure nothing popped up out of the blue for Mr. D. Not trying to keep stalkers or killers at bay."

"And is that still part of your job description here?" asked Zack.

"It is, though he talked about taking it out. Everything seems so low key here. But appearances can be deceptive. Have you all been here a long time?"

"I grew up here," said Logan. "And these two." He nodded toward Austin and Colt.

"And we're relative newcomers," said Luke, pointing at Zack and himself.

"That's cool," said Ivan. "I was concerned when I first arrived here that there might be a divide between the locals and the newcomers. A lot of small towns are like that."

"Nah. Everyone pitches in together here. Everyone's welcoming. Like I told you before, you just need to get to know people."

Colt smiled. "And now you know all of us well enough to come out for a drink. Remind me to give you my number before we leave. If you want a guys' night, I'll be one of your regulars, since these three are all pretty much under the thumb."

Luke shrugged. "I wouldn't put it that way, but with traveling so much for work. When I am here, I tend to spend most of my time with Angel."

"Same here," said Zack.

Logan grinned. "What are you all looking at me for? I'm not going to shrug it off or make some excuse like these two. I am happy to admit that my priority these days is spending time with Roxy. I don't think I could claim to be under the thumb yet. She's still too busy trying not to tie me down. But I'm working on it."

Austin shook his head. "I've known you all my life, and I never thought I'd see the day."

"Me neither," said Colt. "But I'm happy for you. When you finally decided to fall, you fell for a good 'un."

Logan held his gaze for a moment. Colt thought he'd fallen. He sucked in a deep breath. He didn't mean fallen by the wayside or fallen from grace or any other kind of falling. He meant fallen in love. Logan's heart buzzed in his chest when he thought about it and had to admit to himself that Colt was right.

Chapter Fifteen

"Are you meeting up with the guys again tonight?" Roxy called.

Logan stuck his head out of the shower door with a grin. "You tell me. Are you out with the girls?"

She made a face. "Why does what you're doing depend on what I'm doing?"

He shook his head like a big dog, sending drops of water everywhere. "Because you're what I want to do most."

"Sweet talker! Well, I am meeting the girls for dinner. It's a regular thing. Every Thursday." She couldn't help smiling at the sight of his naked body with water running down over it. "You can do me when I get home if you want."

He waggled his eyebrows at her. "I will. And if you're quick, I'll do you now, too. Come on in, the water's wonderful."

She hesitated. "You'll make us late for work."

"Not necessarily." He reached out and tugged at the belt of her robe. It fell open, and she loved the way his gaze traveled over her body. "Come on, you know you want to."

She did. She let the robe fall to the floor and stepped into the shower with him.

He put his hands on her shoulders and kissed her deeply, sending currents of desire racing through her. She tangled her fingers in his hair as he massaged her breasts, first with his hands, then his tongue. That turned her on so much. At first, she'd felt self-conscious about her breasts; they were big and had always been something of a nuisance. Logan had told her repeatedly that they were perfect—and the way he liked to worship them backed up his words.

She gasped as he grazed her nipple with his teeth. "You know these babies are perfect, right?"

She chuckled. Sometimes it felt like he read her mind and had just the right words to reassure her. "I know they are to you, and that's all that matters."

He lifted his head and trapped her body between his and the wall. "That's right. Other guys will think they're perfect, too. But I hope it never matters to you what other guys think."

She was surprised by the intensity in his eyes as his hand found its way between her legs and started to stroke her. She nodded breathlessly.

"Yes?" he asked. "It does matter to you?"

"No," she breathed.

"I want you to be all mine, Roxy."

She closed her fingers around him, loving how hot and hard he was for her. "I am. All yours." She loved the way that sounded. "I want you to be all mine, too." It felt good to say it. She'd finally gotten over her hang-up about not wanting him to feel tied down. If he wanted her, then he needed to be all in with her. She wouldn't settle for less, and she knew now that she didn't have to.

He lifted her leg and wrapped it around his waist with a smile. "I'm all yours, Rox." She felt him pushing at her entrance. "You know I give you everything I've got." As he spoke, he thrust his hips, making her bite down on his shoulder as he filled her.

He began to move, slowly at first, then picking up the pace as he drove deeper and deeper with each thrust. She was at his mercy. She couldn't even keep her own balance, but as she moved with him, their bodies becoming one in a rhythm that had grown so familiar, she realized that she trusted him completely. He wouldn't let her fall. He would give her everything he had, and he'd given her more pleasure than she'd ever known.

As those thoughts filled her head, she felt her body start to come undone. Water ran down over them. His hard body pressed against hers, and his cock felt like the only rock-solid thing in her world. The ball of pleasure that was building in her belly finally exploded, sending waves of pleasure crashing through her. She felt him tense, and his thrusts became even more frantic. He carried her higher and higher until her climax ignited his, and he gasped. She leaned her head back and let go, riding the waves with him until they slowly came back down to earth.

He let her leg slide back down and held her close to his chest as the now-cooling water ran down over them. "You're everything I want, Rox."

Her heart raced. He was everything she wanted, too. For the first time, standing there under the running water, she started to think that maybe he could be her everything. And the thought made her happy.

~ ~ ~

"Come in," Logan called without looking up from his computer.

"Are you busy? Do you want me to come back?" asked Aaron.

"No." Logan finally dragged his eyes away from the screen. "What's up?"

"I need to make a few changes in the schedule. I wanted to run them by you first."

"What changes?"

"I want to finish out Lot Twelve next."

"No. Eleven's next. That's the one they want to use on these site tours for prospective buyers."

"I know. That's what I want to talk to you about. There were some issues with Eleven. It'd make life easier if we can use Twelve." Aaron grinned. "And I figured that since you have some pull with the lady who's arranging the tours ..."

Logan scowled at him. "You want me to use my influence with Roxy to change her schedule?"

"Yeah. I imagine it'd be pretty easy for you to persuade her."

Logan shook his head. "Nope. Not going to happen."

"Why?"

"Because if it were anyone other than Roxy in charge, you'd either talk to them yourself or find a way to make it happen."

"Yeah, but since you have an in, I thought it'd be crazy not to use it."

"Like I said. Not going to happen. What's crazy is you thinking that I'd see scheduling as more important than Roxy. You know what it's taken for me to show her that I'm for real. I'm not going to start manipulating her to get what I want on the work front. She's more important to me than anything that could happen here."

Instead of arguing like Logan had expected, Aaron grinned at him. "That's awesome! Sorry. I thought I was still talking to the old Logan. I know you've hinted at it, but I didn't understand how serious you are about her. Is this it then? Is it the real thing? Are you thinking long-term?"

Logan nodded. His heart raced at the thought, but it was racing with excitement—not fear, which was the effect that the thought of a long-term relationship had always had on him in the past.

Aaron's eyes were wide. "Long, long-term?"

Logan nodded again.

"Like tying the knot and wedding bells and all that shit?"

Logan drew in a deep breath before he nodded this time. "Yeah. Down the line."

Aaron laughed. "Giving yourself a long lead time, so you have a chance to change your mind?"

"No. More like giving myself time to show her that I'm all in. That I'm serious so that when I ask her, she'll say yes."

"Wow! I've never seen a man turn around as fast as you have."

Logan shrugged. "There's no denying that I've sewn enough wild oats for one lifetime. I went hard on being a single guy. Now I'm ready to go hard on being ..." He didn't want to say a *married* guy. Up until this moment, he hadn't even known that that was what he wanted. It was too soon, he knew that. Roxy wouldn't go for it yet. So, saying it out loud felt like tempting fate. "In a real relationship," he finished.

Aaron nodded. "I'm happy for you. I kind of assume that it will happen to all of us at some point, but I didn't expect you to go this willingly—or this fast."

Logan shrugged. "I guess you can never tell. Now, is there anything else you wanted, or can I get back to it?"

"No, that was it. Now I know where you stand, I'll get to work on how we can have Lot Eleven finished up in time."

Logan smirked. "So, you were just looking for an easy way out?"

Aaron shrugged. "That, and I was curious to see how you'd react."

~ ~ ~

"Sorry, I'm late, girls." Maria smiled around at them as she took her seat at the table.

"No worries," said Roxy. "What's the news on this weekend?"

Maria blew out a sigh. "It's off." She shot a look at Angel. "Have you talked to Luke yet?"

"Not yet, no." Angel pulled her phone out of her purse. "Oh, I missed a voicemail from him. I take it they have to fly this weekend."

"Yeah. Clay decided he does need to go to Nashville after all."

"Can't you two still go?" asked Amber.

Maria smiled. "Zack said that we could go with them to Nashville if we want. Clay felt bad about messing up our plans and offered for us to come along for the weekend." She looked at Angel. "That's probably what Luke's message is about. I know I was the one eager to see the snow, but I'm not going to turn down a weekend in Nashville."

Angel smiled. "Me neither. That'll be fun."

Roxy felt a ball of disappointment settle in her stomach. She'd been looking forward to this trip to the mountains. "Do you still want to go?" she asked Amber.

"I can't. I already knew that."

Roxy looked at Kenzie, but she shook her head. "It was never an option for me. It's a busy weekend at the resort."

Roxy blew out a sigh and looked at Maria. "Will you lose the deposit? Do you want us to all chip in and share the cost?"

"No. It's okay. We could have canceled earlier and got the money back; it was me who wanted to wait until the last minute to see if we could make it happen."

Angel looked at Roxy. "You and Logan could still go. It'd be a romantic weekend for just the two of you since it looks like everyone else is dropping out."

Roxy grinned. She liked that idea even more than all of them going together.

"You should go," said Maria. "But talk to him about it tonight and let me know. I want to go ahead and cancel if you're not. They might be able to get a last-minute booking from someone else if I tell them early enough."

"Okay. I'll talk to him as soon as I get home and call you to let you know."

Kenzie raised an eyebrow at her. "And when you say *get home,* you mean to his place? Are you two living together now?"

Roxy shrugged.

"Yes," said Angel firmly. "To all intents and purposes, they are. And if madam here would just wrap her head around it, then I'm sure they could make it official, and she could stop forking out rent money for her place where she hasn't spent a night in weeks."

Roxy looked at her. "I'll admit that I've been dragging my feet about admitting that we're living together. But you really think I'd give up my place?"

"Why wouldn't you?" asked Maria.

Roxy thought about it.

"Because for all she goes on about Logan not being the kind to make a commitment, she's the one who's living with one foot out the door!" said Angel.

"Wow! Say it like you see it, why don't you?" said Roxy.

Angel shrugged. "It's not like I haven't already told you what I think. And I'm sorry I'm being a nag. I know what I think doesn't matter. It's just that I can see what you're putting yourself through—and what you're putting Logan through. He doesn't deserve it."

Roxy was shocked. "What am I putting him through?"

"The poor guy's all in, and you're still only half-hearted about it."

"You really see it that way?"

Maria nodded. "I do. I'm shocked by how much he's changed, but I know he's genuine about it."

"Sorry, Rox, but I'm with them," said Kenzie. "At first, I was ready to rip his balls off if he messed you around. But now I'm feeling more like I want to give you a shake than him. He's for real. Go for it."

Roxy sucked in a big breath and then blew it out again. "So, you're all telling me that I'm screwing this up?"

"Not exactly." Angel gave her a reassuring smile. "Just that you might end up happier if you let yourself trust him."

"And trust yourself," added Kenzie. "Sure, there's a risk you get your heart broken, but even if you do, you'll get over it. You have to put your heart on the line; no risk, no reward."

Roxy thought about it for a long moment. Then she pulled her phone out of her purse and dialed Logan's number.

The others watched her in silence.

"Hey, babe. What's up? Are you finished already?"

"No. We're still having dinner. It's just that I want to ask you something."

"What?"

"Zack and Luke have to fly this weekend, and everyone else is dropping out on the weekend at the cabin. I wondered ..." Her heart was hammering in her chest, but she didn't know what she was afraid of. That he'd say no? That he wouldn't like the idea? He was always telling her that he wanted to spend time with her. She gripped the phone a little tighter. "Do you want to go, anyway? Just you and me."

She held her breath in the few moments before he answered. Was he thinking up an excuse?

"Seriously? I'd love to! That's even better. We'll have a great time. I can't wait."

She laughed. A mixture of relief and happiness that he was so thrilled at the idea. "Great. I'll tell Maria not to cancel the reservation."

"And tell her I'll settle up with Zack later."

She almost argued, wanting to tell him that she'd pay, or that they should at least go halves. But she bit her tongue. They could talk about it later, and she knew the girls would only give her a hard time if she brought it up now. "Okay. I will."

"I'll see you at home."

She smiled that he called it home, too. She liked the idea that he thought she belonged there.

She hung up and looked around at the others.

"Way to go," said Kenzie. "I'll bet he was stoked."

She nodded happily. "He was. Thanks, girls."

Logan couldn't stop smiling on his drive home. He'd enjoyed his evening with the guys, but he couldn't wait for Roxy to get home, and he wanted to be there when she did. She'd taken him by surprise when she'd called to ask if he still wanted to go to the cabin this weekend.

He'd pulled Zack to one side to tell him that he'd pay for the reservation. Zack had been pleased and suggested that some of the others might still go, too, but Logan had set him straight. If they'd all dropped out, then he wanted them to stay that way. He enjoyed everyone's company, but he'd much rather spend the weekend alone with Roxy. He had to admit that the few weekends they'd spent together so far had been low key. Going to the mall, taking walks in the cold and watching football on TV were great. It had shown them both that they did well together in everyday life. But he wanted their life together to hold more fun and adventure, too.

He let himself into the house and turned on the lights. Looking around the living room, he loved all the little signs that a woman lived here. He liked to keep his house clean and tidy, but he wasn't big on knick-knacks or artwork.

She'd bought him a couple of pictures to put on the walls since she claimed it looked like he'd just moved in, even though he'd lived here for years. The flowers he'd bought her stood in a vase on the dining table. They were looking tired. He'd have to get her some more tomorrow. He grinned as he realized it'd be better to wait until Monday—since they'd be away for the weekend.

He went to the door when he heard her car pull into the driveway. His heart raced when she got out and smiled at him.

"Hey." She trotted up the steps to him, and he wrapped her in his arms and dropped a kiss on her lips.

"Hey. Come on in. It's freezing out here."

When they were inside, he followed her to the kitchen, where she opened the fridge and peered inside.

"Are you still hungry? I thought you guys had dinner."

She laughed. "We did. I'm looking for beer."

He laughed. "You didn't get enough to drink?"

"I only had soda because I was driving. Do you want one?"

"Sure. I only had one myself."

She straightened up and handed him a bottle. He popped the top and handed it to her before opening the other. He wanted to talk about going away to the cabin, but he was hoping that she'd bring it up first. He was thrilled that she'd called and asked him but curious what had made her do it.

Once they were settled on the sofa, she put her legs up, and he pulled them across his.

She raised her bottle to him and smiled. "Do you like the idea of us going away together?"

"I love it! It'll be so much better than going with everyone else—and I was looking forward to that."

"That's how I feel, too. I was disappointed when Maria said it was off."

"And you decided that we should go anyway?"

She avoided his gaze, and he felt his heart sink.

"What's up?"

"I have to tell you the truth. I wouldn't have asked you— even though I love the idea. But the girls gave me a hard time."

He frowned, wondering where this was going. "What about?"

"About the fact that I still haven't gone all in with you—even though you have with me."

He smiled. Glad to hear that the other girls were on his side. "You're just taking your time. I know that. I have to earn your trust."

She reached up and planted a kiss on his lips. "You are doing, with everything you say and do. I've been holding back, but it's time for me to meet you halfway. I need to be honest with you." She took a deep breath. "I love living here with you."

He grinned. "Thanks for saying it. You can stay as long as you want."

"I want."

His heart raced, and he searched her face. She was smiling, and she nodded as if she were saying yes in advance to the question he had to ask next. "You want to live with me?"

She nodded. "I do."

A rush of adrenaline coursed through his veins at the sound of those two words. He loved that she'd said that about living with him—and one day, he hoped they'd repeat them about wanting to make the arrangement permanent.

He closed his arms around her. "Thank you."

She looked up into his eyes. "Thank you. I'm sorry I've been wishy-washy about it."

He shook his head. "Don't be. I think that given my history, it's only fair that I should be the one to go out on a limb and hope that you'll go with me. I don't mind putting myself up to be shot down. I know you could break my heart, but it's a risk worth taking."

She cupped his cheek in her hand. "I'd never do that."

He turned and kissed her palm. "I hope not, but I need you to know that my heart is on the line here."

She raised an eyebrow.

"I'm messing this up. What I'm trying to say is that I love you, Roxy."

"Oh." She looked so adorable, her eyes wide with surprise, and her mouth open in a perfect little O shape that filled his mind with thoughts of what they could do later.

She pressed her lips together, and he placed a finger over them. "You don't need to say anything. I just wanted you to know."

Chapter Sixteen

"Do you want me to take your bag out to the truck?"

Roxy laughed at Logan, who was standing in the doorway waiting. She was sitting at the island in the kitchen, finishing her coffee.

"Are you trying to tell me to hurry my ass up?"

He laughed with her. "No. I wouldn't do that. I'm just trying to get things ready."

She nodded and smirked at him. "I would have thought that you were someone who just threw things together at the last minute and went."

"I am. It's just that what I consider to be the last minute already came and went."

She laughed. "And now you're waiting for me. Don't worry. My bag's ready. She nodded to where it was sitting by the door. And since you're such a heathen that you won't even take the time to enjoy a leisurely cup of coffee before we go, I'll put this in a travel mug and get my coat."

She got to her feet, and he came to close his arms around her. "I'm not trying to rush you. We can sit and drink coffee if that's what you want to do."

"We can drink it on the way. I'll grab you a travel mug, too." She stepped away from him to get the mugs ready.

"Thanks. I'm just excited to get going."

"I am, too. I've never been up there. Do you have the directions?"

"I've already plugged the address into the GPS."

"Wow. Aren't you on the ball?! Okay. I have the coffees and my purse. If you want to grab my bag, we can go."

It was a beautiful drive and a sunny, but cold day. She stared out of the window when he turned off Route Twenty onto a smaller highway that climbed up ahead of them.

"It's so pretty up here."

"It is. I love it. We used to come up here all the time as kids."

"Your family?"

"No. I used to come with Colt and his family."

"I love that you two have that—that you've been friends all your lives and are still so close."

"Yeah. He's like a brother. We don't do much together these days, other than meeting up for a drink now and then, but it doesn't matter."

Roxy bit her lip and then decided to say it anyway. "We should invite him over for dinner one night. I like Colt. He and I have always gotten along well."

Logan turned and grinned at her. "That'd be great. I'd like that."

"Good. I think we need to find a way to manage our time."

She could see his eyebrows knit together as he drove. "What do you mean?"

She laughed. "Nothing as anal as that sounded. I mean, I'm excited that we get this weekend to ourselves, and I love the time we hang out just the two of us, but we need to figure out what we do with girls' nights and guys' nights and couples' nights, and I don't like the idea of us not hanging out with our single friends. Angel and Luke and Maria and Zack made the effort to include me still. It's felt awkward sometimes, but I like it, too. I get to see them in the new lives that they're living." She made a face. "I'm rambling, and I'm not sure I'm explaining myself very well."

He reached across and gave her hand a squeeze. "It makes sense to me. You want to know which part I like the best?"

"Which?"

"The part where you don't want to leave our friends out of this new life of ours. I like that you don't want to leave them out, but I like it even better that you're seeing it as our new life. That's what I want it to be, Rox."

She nodded. She did, too. She loved the idea. She just needed a little time to get used to it. She was trying to catch herself whenever she realized that she was focusing on how the old Logan might feel. She needed to let that go, and she was doing a better job of taking him at his word. Her heart fluttered in her chest. She still wasn't letting herself think too hard about the three little words he'd said to her the other night. She couldn't process that yet, at least, she didn't want to. She knew that when she did, she'd have to admit to herself and to him, that she'd gone and fallen in love with him, too. She felt that her saying it back would take them past a point of no return. She smiled as she realized that was exactly how it would be. It'd be making a commitment—and Logan had already done it.

The road rose more steeply after a while, and the trees crowded in thicker and taller.

"Are we nearly there yet?" she asked.

Logan laughed. "You're like a little kid. What's up? Do you have to pee?"

She laughed with him. "No. I'm just excited." She rolled her window down a little way and sniffed the cold air. "You can smell the snow. There's something magical about snow. It's all sparkly and pretty." She rolled the window back up with a shiver.

"It's also damned cold. I hope you brought lots of warm things."

"I did. I told you. I used to ski. I dug out my old clothes."

When they rounded the next turn in the road, she saw the snow. "Wow. Look at that. A minute ago, there was nothing on the ground, and there's a couple of inches here."

"It's always been that way here. When I was a kid, I was disappointed every time that there was no snow. Colt's dad would tell me to be patient, and every time when we turned that corner, there it was."

"Aww. I'll bet you were really cute as a kid."

He laughed. "I don't think anyone ever called me cute. I was a little rascal. Always in trouble for something."

She laughed. "You've not changed much then."

He shot her a mock hurt look. "I haven't gotten myself in any kind of trouble for a long time. Definitely not since I met you."

She waggled her eyebrows at him. "Maybe I'll get you in trouble this weekend."

"I like the sound of that. What kind of trouble do you have in mind?"

"Oh, I'm sure I'll think if something."

He winked at her. "I think nudity and indecent behavior in a public place are out of the question this weekend—it's too damned cold. But I'll bring you back in the summer, and we can go for those then."

Her tummy flipped over at the thought. He was talking about them having sex outside? Her body reacted just as strongly as if he'd said he was going to pull the truck over so that they could do it now. She could feel her stiff nipples chafe against her bra. Heat pooled between her legs, and she pressed her thighs together.

Logan raised an eyebrow at her. "You like that idea?"

She nodded breathlessly, surprised at just how much she liked it.

"In that case … It might be cold out there, but I'm sure we could come up with something."

She loved the eager look on his face when she said, "I think we should."

"You like it outside, huh?"

She could feel the heat in her cheeks, but she had to tell him. "I don't know, but I like the idea."

He reached over and rested his hand on her thigh—which only served to intensify the heat between her legs. "So, you want me to be your first?"

She nodded. For some reason, the way he phrased it made her even hornier. She loved the idea of him being her first—outdoors or anywhere else.

"Your wish is my command."

She grinned. "What are you going to do?"

"Make it special. Your first time should always be special."

Logan started to get a little concerned as he followed the gravel driveway. It'd been a couple of minutes since they'd turned off the main road, and there was still no cabin in sight. Navigation systems were notorious for being way off up here in the mountains. He started to look for a place to turn around. Then they rounded the corner, and he heard Roxy gasp beside him.

"Oh, look, Logan. It's beautiful!"

She was right. Zack had sent him a link to the online listing for the place, and the cabin was as nice as he'd expected. What he hadn't expected was the breathtaking view. There had been some photos online, but he'd assumed that they were taken around the area—not right from the cabin. It stood in a clearing on the slope of the mountain and laid out before it was a beautiful valley ringed by snowy peaks.

"It is," he agreed as he brought the truck to a stop.

Roxy was out the door and ran through the snow to the deck, which led out in front of the cabin. He hurried after her eager to look out from there. He put his arm around her shoulders, and she leaned her head against him as they stood and took it all in. He didn't feel like words were necessary. It was just so damned beautiful. It felt like a special moment to take in that view with her.

The sun shone down, making the snow sparkle, just as she'd described earlier. And he had to agree—it did feel like there was something magical about it. Though, whether that was the snow or the woman standing by his side, he wasn't sure.

After a while, he felt her shiver and hugged her closer. "Come on. Let's get the bags inside. The view will be just the same from in there, and we'll be warmer."

Once they'd brought everything inside, they explored the cabin. It was huge. Way more than they needed with its five bedrooms. He was glad that four of them would remain empty.

Roxy stopped when they came out of the fourth one and frowned. "Which bedroom shall we take?"

Logan had read the description of the place, and he already knew. He took hold of her hand and led her to a doorway at the end of the hall. It opened to a second set of stairs, and he led her up to the third floor.

"This is amazing!" She grinned at him. "It might be two sets of stairs, but we could easily spend all weekend up here."

He laughed and went to sit on the bed, patting the space beside him for her to join him. "I wouldn't have a problem with that."

The bedroom was a huge loft. The front wall was all glass, giving them an even more incredible view of the valley and mountain ranges stretching for miles into the distance. The inside was equally impressive. The bed was a fourposter, which gave Logan a couple of ideas.

Roxy got to her feet and went into the bathroom. "You have to see this."

He went to join her and laughed when he saw the oversized tub, which looked like it would comfortably fit four people, let alone just the two of them. The shower looked more like a shower room than a stall. It had six showerheads, and what looked to Logan like steam nozzles, too.

He grinned at her. "I'm guessing we'll be squeaky clean by the time we leave."

"We will. I was so excited to explore this area, but now I doubt we'll even leave the bedroom, let alone the cabin."

He raised an eyebrow at her. "I thought you wanted to ski?"

She shrugged and gave him a wicked smile. "We'll have to see if we have the energy for it."

"I won't be disappointed if we don't go anywhere else. We can always come back another time."

She smiled. "I'd like that. I can see this becoming a regular haunt."

His heart buzzed in his chest. Hearing her say that gave him hope. He knew he got carried away sometimes thinking about the future and what it might hold for them. Every time she said something that indicated she was thinking about them long-term made him feel that he wasn't setting himself up for a fall. He had to believe that she felt it, that she wanted it, too. She was being more cautious than he was, that was all.

"I suppose we'd better go and unpack the cooler and see if we have everything we need. If we need to venture back down the mountain for supplies, I'd rather figure that out now. I don't like the idea of driving on those roads in the dark."

"Yeah. Let's go and get unpacked, and then we can decide what I'm going to do to you?"

She raised an eyebrow, and he laughed.

"Sorry, I meant what we're going to do."

After they'd unpacked all the supplies they'd brought and explored the kitchen, it was clear that they wouldn't need to go out in search of groceries.

Roxy laughed as she pulled the last packet of chips out. "I know you said you were going to make sure we had everything we might need. But were you planning for us to sit here and eat all weekend? Even if we ate non-stop, I don't think we'd get through all the goodies you brought."

He shrugged. "I'd rather have it and not need it than need it and not have it. This way, we don't need to use up any of our time going grocery shopping."

"True. I'm not complaining. I'm impressed."

"I'm glad to hear it. Do you want me to impress you with my skiing abilities, too? It might be busy on a Saturday afternoon, but we can go and check out the resort if you'd like. They have rental equipment."

"Yeah. Let's go out and explore. I don't want to waste all our time in line waiting for a ski lift if it's busy. But we can at least scope the place out for another visit."

When they got there, the ski resort was heaving with people. It took Logan a good five minutes just to find a space in the parking lot.

Roxy made a face at him when he cut the engine. "I don't like our chances of getting to ski, do you?"

He shook his head. "No. But now that we're here, we can have a wander around. See what the place is like these days. I haven't been here for years. And if you want to do some people watching, we can sit and have a hot chocolate."

"Ooh. Yes. Let's do that."

He took her hand as they walked across the parking lot, and she smiled up at him. "This is wonderful. I'm so glad we came."

"I am, too. We should do what you said and make it a regular thing. If we plan better, we can come up on Friday night and be first here and out on the slopes on Saturday morning."

"Yeah, we should do that. The early bird gets the powder."

"That's true. And it looks like the late birds won't even get a seat to watch." They'd reached the main area near the bottom of the ski lifts. A long line waited at the bottom. Another line stretched out through the doors of the rental shop. The large terrace outside the café was heaving with people. Logan couldn't see a single empty seat. Some people were sitting on the floor leaning back against the wall, and others were leaning on the railing to enjoy their drinks and the view.

Roxy made a face. "Jeez. I thought it'd be busy, but this place is a zoo."

"Do you want to try for a hot chocolate?"

"No." She looked so disappointed, he felt bad.

"Don't worry, we knew this might happen." He tugged on her hand and started heading back to the truck. "This isn't our only option."

"There's another ski resort?"

"No, but there's a place I'd like to show you. I think you'll like it. And we should be able to get hot chocolate there."

Chapter Seventeen

"Where are we going?" Roxy asked as he pulled out of the parking lot, and another truck pulled into his space immediately.

"Wait and see."

"Do I have to wait long?"

He laughed. "You really are like a little kid, aren't you? Hold tight. It's only about ten minutes from here."

When he reached the bottom of the mountain, he glanced over at her, wanting to see her reaction when they came into town.

"Oh, it's like a fairy tale!" she exclaimed.

He chuckled. "I don't know about that, but they always do a great job of decorating around here for the holidays."

He drove down Main Street of the small tourist town, glancing at all the Christmas decorations as they went. He knew it would look even better after dark, but at least this was making up for her disappointment about the crowded ski resort. The town was busy, with lots of people on the sidewalk window-shopping and even sitting in the pavement cafes despite the cold.

"Can we explore?" Roxy asked.

"Of course, we can. That's what we're here for, and to get that hot chocolate."

He drove the length of Main without finding a space and ended up two blocks over. Roxy took his hand as they walked back. "This is so cool. I didn't even know about this place."

"And you've lived at the lake for how long? Haven't you explored the area at all?"

She shrugged. "Not really. I was getting to know Summer Lake itself at first; there's so much to do there. I've thought about getting out to see what else is out here, but I haven't had much time—or anyone to go with. It's hard to coordinate weekends off with the girls. We all usually work at least one day."

He smiled. "Now you have someone to explore with. There are a lot of cool towns around here. We should make a list and go see them all."

She stopped walking and reached up to plant a kiss on his lips.

"What was that for?" he asked with a grin.

"Just for being so wonderful. I've kind of wished I had a boyfriend. I've wished that I could get out and get to know the area. You're granting all my wishes."

He laughed. "You make me sound like a fairy."

"Hmm. No. I can't see you in a sparkly outfit with a wand."

"I promise you; you won't ever see that."

When they got back on Main, Roxy looked around like a kid in a candy store. "It's so pretty! Look at all the lights strung across the road, and all the storefronts are decorated. Oh, Logan, I love it!"

His heart raced. For a moment there he'd imagined that her last word was *you*. The disappointment that settled in his stomach when he realized his mistake only served to remind him how much he was hoping to hear that—to know that she felt the same way he did.

"Isn't it great?" He hoped she couldn't hear the disappointment in his voice. He needn't have worried; she was dragging him toward a store where there was a Christmas tree set up in the window complete with twinkling lights and a line of dancing elves.

She laughed. "Aww, look. The little elves are so cute."

He smiled through pursed lips. He could see her point, but he could also see that he was in for a long afternoon.

~ ~ ~

"What can I get you?"

Roxy looked up at the server with a smile. "I'll take an extra-large hot chocolate with whipped cream and candy cane."

Logan looked up from his menu and raised an eyebrow.

"And for you?"

"Just a straight hot chocolate."

"Give him the whipped cream and candy cane, too," said Roxy.

The girl smiled and turned to leave.

Logan laughed. "How do you know that I even like candy canes and whipped cream? I could be allergic to them for all you know."

"You're not, though, are you? Everyone loves candy canes, and for all the quips you've made about wanting to bring whipped cream into the bedroom, I know you must like it."

"Now there's an idea. We should pick up a can of cream on the way back. I can tie you to that bed and eat cream off you."

Roxy felt the heat in her cheeks. She liked the sound of that. She glanced around, wondering if anyone had heard what he said. "That sounds like fun."

"It will be." He smiled. "Though I'm not sure you'll think it's as fun as this afternoon has been. I didn't know you were such a Christmas freak." He nodded toward the bags around her feet.

"I can't help it. I love it. All the decorations and the music and the movies—"

He groaned.

"What's wrong?"

"Are you telling me that I'm going to have to watch Christmas movies for the next several weeks?"

She shrugged. "You don't have to."

"I think I do. See, I was planning to ask you if you're going to stay?"

She nodded happily. "I'd love to. It'll be our first Christmas together. We can get a tree and bake cookies and ..." Suddenly, she realized what she was doing and stopped short. She didn't want to scare him by painting a scene of happy domesticity that might scare him. She met his gaze. "Sorry, I ..."

He grinned and reached across the table for her hand. "Don't be sorry. It sounds wonderful. I'll put up with the sappy Christmas music if I get to share Christmas with you."

"Aww," she squeezed his hand. "Thank you."

The server came back and set two mugs down in front of them.

Logan looked at his. It was a huge mug with a tower of whipped cream on top with candy canes hooked all around the rim. He looked up at Roxy. "Seriously?"

"Yep!" She pulled a candy cane out of her own and scooped up some whipped cream with it before offering it to him.

He grinned and licked the cream off it. "Mm. That is good."

She laughed. "I told you." She watched as he pulled two of the canes from his own mug. "No, don't just eat them, you need to let them melt into the chocolate, so you get all the flavors together."

"I wasn't going to eat them." He carefully put the two canes on top of her whipped cream, arranged in the shape of a heart. "I just wanted you to know." He pointed at his eye, then at the candy cane heart and then at her.

Roxy felt tears well up in her eyes and reached for his hand again. She'd been planning to tell him this weekend. She'd wanted to find the perfect moment—maybe in bed, or in front of the fire, or looking out at that amazing view. But he'd chosen the moment for her. She couldn't let it go by. "I love you, too, Logan."

His eyes widened, and he gripped her hand tightly as a big smile spread across his face. "You do?"

"I do. I didn't know when to tell you—or how—but I can't wait any longer. I've gone and fallen in love with you."

He got up and leaned across the table to plant a kiss on her lips. "I love you with all my heart, Rox. You're my person."

She let out a little sound that was half laugh half cry as tears welled up again. "I'm your person?"

"Yeah. They say there's someone for everyone. I never bought into that. I do now. You're it for me."

She smiled through the tears that were threatening to spill down her cheeks. "I thought I'd find my person someday, but I never thought that you'd be him—that you'd want to be."

"I want to be. Today, tomorrow and always."

"Aww." She squeezed his hand tighter. "You're a romantic at heart, aren't you?"

He swaggered his shoulders. "I never thought I was, but you seem to bring it out in me."

It was almost dark by the time they'd finished wandering through the stores. Logan would have happily been done after their hot chocolate break, but on their way back to the truck, Roxy had pointed out a souvenir Christmas decoration made in the shape of a candy cane heart in a store window. Remembering how good it had felt when she told him that he was a romantic at heart, he'd gone inside and bought it.

"It'll go on our tree," he'd told her with a smile.

She hadn't replied, but the smile on her face had been worth the extra hour that they'd spent browsing the stores again afterward. He'd sneakily picked up a leaflet in the café when he'd gone in to pay. He'd thought he might surprise her with it tomorrow, but now that it was dark, he decided that it'd be better to do it tonight. She loved the lights, just as he'd expected.

Once they'd piled all the bags into the back of the cab, she opened the passenger door to get in.

"Where are you going?" he asked.

She gave him a puzzled look. "I thought we were going back."

"Not yet. There's one more thing I want to check out." He held his hand out to her. "Do you want to see?"

She laughed. "Of course, I do! You know how much I'm loving this."

He kept his fingers crossed in his pocket as they walked to the end of the block and then turned right away from Main Street.

"Where are we going?"

"Wait and see."

A wave of relief rushed through him when they reached the square in front of the town hall. There was an archway of Christmas lights and lined up beyond it were three horse-drawn carriages that were also adorned with lights.

Roxy looked up at him. "Can we?!"

He laughed. "That's why we're here."

She was as eager as a small child dragging him toward them. "Come on. Those people look like they're going over there, too. I want to get the white horse – the first one."

Logan laughed as he hurried after her.

Once they were seated in the carriage with a blanket over their laps, he put his arm around her shoulders and dropped a kiss on her lips.

"This is so perfect. Thank you. I can't believe we're doing this. I've always wanted to go on a sleigh ride."

He laughed. "It's not quite a sleigh ride—"

She put a finger to his lips. "Don't spoil it. To me, it's a sleigh ride."

"Okay. Whatever you say."

She leaned her head against his shoulder. "I say this is the most magical day of my life. I'm with my hot sexy boyfriend, we're planning our first Christmas together, and he's taking me on a sleigh ride."

He grinned, loving her enthusiasm about it all, and most of all, loving the way she said their *first* Christmas together, as if she, too, were starting to believe in their future.

The horses turned onto Main Street, and Roxy looked all around, taking in the lights and the music that was now playing from somewhere. She grinned at him. "You know, when I lived in the city, I used to daydream about going away for Christmas, going somewhere like this, some small town where Christmas is still magical. In the city, it's all about the bottom line. How much merchandise can they shift in the month of December, or these days it starts as soon as Halloween is over."

Logan didn't like to say that the business owners here didn't go to all this effort purely out of a sense of community. They were liking turning a nice profit, too.

She made a face at him as if she'd read his mind. "I know! But what I'm saying is that this is my ideal, my too good to be true—except it is true, you made it come true for me. "I love you, Logan."

He closed his arms around her and claimed her mouth in a kiss. "I love you. Rox," he murmured when he finally lifted his head.

"Can't we just stay here?" asked Roxy when they were getting ready to leave the cabin on Sunday. "I don't want to go back to work. I want to stay and pretend it's Christmas until it really is Christmas."

Logan laughed. "Sorry. I know you think it's magical here, but the magic runs out in about an hour. We have to check out by two."

She sighed. "I know. I just don't want it to end."

"We'll come back. I'll check the availability as soon as we get home and we can book for whenever you can get off work."

She nodded. "I hope we can. I'd like to come back before Christmas."

He laughed and looked at all the shopping bags from yesterday that were piled up with their luggage, waiting to be taken out to the truck. "What you don't think you bought enough?"

"I'll buy more if we do come, but it's not that. This place feels special to me now."

He hugged her to him. "It feels special to me, too." He knew it always would. It was the place where she first told him that she loved him. "We should make it a tradition that we come here every year in the run up to Christmas."

She looked up at him, and for a moment, he worried that he shouldn't have said that, but she smiled. "I think we should. I'll drive you nuts with Christmas shopping and then make it up to you in that fourposter bed afterward, just like last night."

He held her a little tighter. "If you're promising me repeat performances of last night, we can come here every weekend!"

She laughed. "What time is it?"

He checked his watch. "Ten after one."

She waggled her eyebrows. "Do you want a repeat before we leave?"

His cock sprang to attention at the thought. Part of him knew he should say no, but that part was weak. They could still check out on time. He took hold of her hand and led her toward the stairs. "I'll never say no to that."

When they reached the bedroom, she put a hand to his shoulder and pushed him so that he sat down on the bed. He pulled his shirt up and off and started to unfasten his jeans, but his hands forgot what they were doing and fell still in his lap as he watched her unfasten her top and then reach around to unhook her bra. He couldn't wait for her breasts to be free, out for him to see and to touch. They really were the perfect breasts as far as he was concerned. He'd done everything he could to convince her of that—everything except remind her that he'd had plenty to compare them to.

Roxy loved the way he watched her. She'd grown in confidence since that first time he'd made love to her. She didn't wait for him to undress her anymore. She knew he loved to watch her undress herself.

As soon as she unfastened her bra, his gaze was fixed on her breasts, and she doubted it would leave them, no matter what else she did. She let the bra fall to the floor and smiled to herself as she caressed her nipples with her hands.

A low groan escaped his lips. "I want to tell you that I should be the one doing that, but—man!—watching you is almost as good."

"Only almost?" She circled her nipple with her thumb and shuddered, both from the way it felt and the lust in his eyes as he watched.

He groaned again. "I dunno, Rox. Come here. Maybe you should touch one, and I'll have the other."

She went to the bed and kneeled over him, straddling him and loving the feel of rough denim brushing between her thighs. She leaned over him, dangling one breast in front of his face. "Like this?"

She gasped as he took her in his mouth and sucked hard. Electric currents went zapping from his lips through her breast all the way to the place between her legs where his hard cock was now pressing.

She let her head fall back and let him take charge of both breasts, his hands and lips working her into a frenzy. She started to rock in his lap, still enjoying the feel of the denim but starting to need to remove it.

She stopped when his hands stilled. He'd had one on each breast, but now he put them both on her left and started to touch in a way that felt more clinical than sexual.

"What are you doing?"

"I don't know. I just felt something."

She laughed. "I was feeling something, too." She rocked her hips again. "Let's get back to it."

"Hold on a minute, Rox … there."

He pressed his finger against the side of her breast, and she winced. "Ouch!" That wasn't nice."

He looked up at her. "I'm sorry. I didn't mean to hurt you."

"It didn't hurt. It's just tender. That's not the kind of touching we're doing here."

He was frowning. "Have you felt that before?"

"No." She blew out a sigh. She didn't want to examine the imperfections of her body right now. She'd rather explore the perfection of his.

"Seriously, Rox." He took hold of her hand and placed it over the spot where he'd touched. "See if you can feel it."

She half-heartedly pressed around, then shook her head. "Nope. But that doesn't surprise me. Breasts are made up of fatty tissue. They're not going to be perfectly smooth."

He slid her off his lap, looking serious. "I'm not talking about them not being smooth. I'm worried about what that might be."

"It's nothing." She frowned. "Well, it's a mood killer, I'll say that."

He put his arm around her shoulders. "I'm sorry, babe. I didn't mean to ruin the moment, but that scares me."

"It shouldn't. It's nothing."

"How do you know that?"

She shrugged and touched the area again, starting to wonder if he might be right. Her fingers found a small hard lump, and she frowned. "Breast tissue is lumpy." She said—telling herself as much as him.

"But now you can feel it, and you're not so sure yourself, are you?"

"I'm sure it's nothing."

"Will you promise me you'll go to the doctor tomorrow and get it checked out?"

"I promise I'll go, but it won't be tomorrow. I'm at work. I'll call and see when I can get an appointment."

He scowled. "If you don't make an appointment, I'll make one for you."

She stared at him indignantly and opened her mouth to ask what right he thought he had, but it hit her before she spoke. He believed he had the right because he cared.

Tears welled up in her eyes.

"Hey! Don't be scared. I'm sure it'll turn out to be nothing."

She shook her head as he wrapped his arm around her. "The tears aren't about being scared—I just understood how much you care."

He nodded solemnly. "I told you, Rox. I love you. I want to take care of you. In every way."

She sniffed and got up. She collected her top and bra from the floor and started to put them back on.

He pulled his shirt back on and gave her a rueful smile. "And you thought I was the kind of guy who was just looking to get laid."

"Yeah. In this one instance, I wish I was right."

"I'm sorry. I'll make it up to you. That's more important, though." He was staring at her breasts again, but this time instead of lust, his eyes were filled with concern.

Chapter Eighteen

"Promise you'll call me after you've made your doctor's appointment; let me know when it is?"

"Only if you promise me that you'll stop worrying about it. I'm sure it's nothing." Roxy leaned across the console and pecked his lips.

"If it's nothing, then there's no reason for you to put off getting it checked out, is there?"

She nodded reluctantly. "Okay, okay. I'll do it. I'm just mad at the stupid lump. I hate that it brought our lovely weekend to such an abrupt end."

"Me, too, Rox. But I'm glad I found it. If it is something … something that needs attention, then the sooner they get started, the better."

"Yeah, but another hour in that bed wouldn't have changed anything." She smiled, wanting to get away from the subject. She was sure it was nothing, but it had hung over them all the way home yesterday, and last night, too. He kept worrying about it.

"We'll go back. I'll check the availability on the calendar when I get into work."

"Okay. Speaking of getting into work, that's what I should do. What time do you think you'll be finished?"

"I can get off at five if you can?"

"I'll try. I'll let you know." She ran her tongue over her bottom lip and gave him what she hoped was a seductive smile. "Maybe tonight we can get back to what we were doing before you found that thing."

He smiled, but she could tell his heart wasn't in it. "We will, but only—"

She rolled her eyes. "Only if I've made an appointment to see the doctor, right?"

He gave her an apologetic smile. "I'm sorry, Rox. I love you. I need to know that you're okay."

"Okay. I'm going in now. I'll make the damned appointment and text you when it's done."

He caught her arm as she turned to open the truck door. "Don't be mad at me. Please?"

She softened. How could she be mad at this gorgeous man who was only being a pain in the ass because he cared about her so much. "I'm not. I'm sorry. I know you mean well." She brought his hand up to her lips and kissed the back of it. "I'll see you tonight."

When she got to her office, she set her purse down on the desk with a sigh.

"Uh-oh. That doesn't sound too promising."

She turned, startled by Angel's voice. She hadn't seen her standing over by the printer.

"Is everything okay? How was your weekend?"

"The weekend was great. How about you? How was Nashville?"

"We had an amazing time. What's up with you? I thought you'd be all sunshine and smiles after your weekend in the snow with sexy Logan."

Roxy smiled. "Sexy Logan was amazing. The cabin was gorgeous. We took a ride up to the ski resort, but it was way too crowded to be any fun. So, we visited Stanton Falls. Have you ever been there?"

"No! But I want to. I heard that they go overboard on Christmas up there. Was it Christmassy, or is it too early for that?"

Roxy grinned. "It was like Christmas gone wild! It was amazing, Angel. You know what I'm like, I love Christmas. And Logan was so sweet. He went into all the stores with me; he even bought a special Christmas decoration. And he took me on a sleigh ride."

"A sleigh ride? They're doing those already?"

Roxy laughed. "Not exactly. It's a horse-drawn carriage with Christmas lights that goes through the town, but still."

Angel smiled. "It sounds wonderful. Very romantic. But if it was such a good time, why did you seem so down when you came in?"

Roxy shrugged. "It kind of ended a little abruptly."

"Oh, no! Why? Did you fight?"

"No. Nothing like that." She smiled. "Quite the opposite, in fact. We were … fooling around, and he felt something in my boob."

"A lump?"

"Yeah, but I'm sure it's nothing."

"Maybe, but you should get it checked right away. You can never be too careful." She looked thoughtful. "Did it scare Logan off?"

"No. It's got him worried." She smiled. "I was more concerned that it killed the mood, and he was all worried about me. He insisted I get it checked. I thought he was being bossy at first, and then I realized—it's because he cares about me. He really cares about me, Angel."

"Anyone with eyes in their head can see that. I'm surprised he hasn't professed his undying love for you yet."

Roxy dropped her gaze.

"He has! Hasn't he?"

"He says he loves me. And he talks about the future. When he bought that decoration, he said it was starting a Christmas tradition."

"Aww." Angel clasped her hands together. "I'll bet he's just a big old softie underneath. He has a big heart."

"He has. I …" Her phone buzzed, and she fished it out of her purse.

"Is that him?"

"Yeah. Checking to see if I made an appointment yet."

"Get on the phone and do it now. I'll get us some coffee."

Roxy dialed the number and waited while it rang. She'd only been to the doctor's twice since she moved here. Dr. Morgan—Michael—was cool. She liked him. But she didn't like the idea of him messing with her boobs. She'd heard that there was a new lady doctor. Hopefully, she'd be able to get in with her.

"Summer Lake Medical Center. This is Abbie speaking. How can I help you?"

"Hi, Abbie. This is Roxy Buchanon. I'd like to make an appointment with the new doctor."

"Doctor Stevens is out of town this week. Would you like to wait? If you want to see Dr. Morgan, he just had a cancellation for nine tomorrow morning."

Roxy blew out a sigh. She didn't know which was worse.

"Is everything okay?"

Roxy pursed her lips. She'd met Abbie a couple of times. She was nice. She wasn't sure she wanted to explain her dilemma to her, though. "Can you hold that nine a.m. for me for a little while?"

"Okay, but call me back and let me know within the hour, would you? I don't want to hold it for too long if you don't need it."

"I will."

Roxy hung up just as Angel was coming back in with the coffees.

"Did you get an appointment?"

"No. I …" Her phone rang. And she knew before she looked that it was Logan.

"I just called the doctor's office." She answered, without bothering to say hello.

He chuckled. "Sorry. When's your appointment?"

She made a face at Angel. She didn't need this. She'd rather not bother at all. "I don't have one yet. The new woman, Dr. Stevens, is out till next week. So, now I have to decide between enduring a week of you pestering about it, or letting Michael handle my boobs."

"When can you get in with Michael?"

"Tomorrow morning."

"Then I'd say do it. The sooner, the better."

If Angel hadn't been in the office with her, she might have asked how he felt about some other guy messing with her boobs. But the fact that he didn't even mention it told her just how concerned he was.

"Do you feel comfortable with him?"

"Yeah. It's fine. I'll call them back now."

"Okay. Good. Sorry, babe. I just can't help worrying. You've only just come into my life. I can't stand to think about something bad happening to you."

"It won't."

"Not if you get it taken care of straight away."

"No. I'll see you later."

"Love you."

"I love you, too."

When she hung up, Angel was beaming at her.

"What?"

"Nothing. I'm keeping my mouth shut. I will tell you that Logan has gone up in my estimation. That's all. Now you call back and make your appointment, and then I'll get off your case. We won't know if there's any point in worrying until you've been in."

"Exactly. I wish you'd tell Logan that!"

~ ~ ~

Logan paced his office. He couldn't make himself sit at his
desk and focus on anything. He glanced at the clock. Nine-ten.
Roxy should be in with Michael now. He wished she'd let him
go with her, but she'd insisted that she wanted to go by herself.
He'd had an eight o'clock meeting scheduled with one of the
suppliers this morning, and she'd told him he should keep it.
He'd canceled it anyway. There was no way he would have
been any use. He was too worried about her. He didn't know
much about breast cancer—though he knew a hell of a lot
more now than he had on Sunday morning. He'd spent most
of his time researching it online. Hopefully, Roxy was right,
and he was blowing things out of proportion. From what he'd
read, breast tissue was naturally lumpy tissue. But he'd swear
that lump hadn't been there before. He should know. He'd
gotten to know her breasts very well over the last few weeks.

"Hey!"

He started when Nate appeared in the doorway. "What's
going on? I thought you were meeting with Saunders this
morning."

"I had to cancel it. We're going to reschedule later in the
week."

Nate frowned and came into the office. "Why? Is there
anything I need to know about?"

"No. It's all good. You know I like to stay ahead of the
game. There's nothing urgent about the meeting."

"Okay. And why the need to cancel? What else is going on?
Did you need the time to put out fires somewhere else?"

Logan shook his head. "Nope. Everything's great."

Nate gave him an enquiring look. "So, why not just tell me
why you canceled?"

Logan pursed his lips.

"Does that explain why you look like crap?"

"I suppose."

"Something up with you and Roxy?"

He blew out a sigh. "Not with us, just with her. You have to pretend I haven't told you this. I doubt she'd want you, or anyone else, to know."

"I won't say a word, and you don't have to tell me if you don't want. I can respect that it's none of my business."

"It's not, but now that you're here, I need to talk about it. I'm driving myself freaking nuts."

"So, tell me."

"She's at the doctor's this morning getting a lump in her breast checked out."

"Oh! Damn. You shouldn't have come in. You should have gone with her."

"She didn't want me. She thinks I'm making a fuss about nothing."

"You might well be. A lot of lumps turn out to be nothing."

"I hope I am. But I can't stop all the thoughts going around in my head. What if it's bad? What if she has to go through treatment, surgery?"

"Then she'll go through it, and she'll come out the other side fine. My mom did. Lots of people do these days."

"Your mom had breast cancer?"

"Yeah. That was some scary shit. But she's a fighter. She was determined that she was going to beat it, and she did." Nate smiled. "I reckon Roxy would be the same. She strikes me as someone who's pretty determined. I know not everyone wins the battle, but I'll tell you my mom and her group of *warriors* as she calls them are some kickass women."

Logan nodded. He was glad to hear that Nate's mom had won her battle. It made him feel a little bit better, though he was hoping that Roxy wouldn't have a battle to fight.

Nate grasped his shoulder. "Why don't you get out of here? Go meet up with her. What time's her appointment?"

"She should be in there right now. She won't thank me if I show up. She said she'll call me when she's done, and then she's coming over here to work anyway."

"I think you should go meet her when she comes out. Is she seeing Michael?"

Logan's heart raced. "Shit. Now you've got me scared. Why do you say that?"

"Only because I remember so vividly every detail of what happened with my mom. I went with her because I was home visiting, and it'd been such a long time since I'd been back that she wanted me to spend every minute I could with her." He smiled. "We were going to see an afternoon movie, and she told me she had a quick checkup appointment that she needed to stop at on the way to the movie theater. I didn't know what it was for. But I'll never forget the look on her face when she came out. The doctor sent her straight to the hospital for a biopsy."

He gave Logan an apologetic smile. "Hopefully, Roxy will be mad at you for being there when she comes out of her appointment. But if Michael sends her straight to the hospital, she might just be happy to see you."

Logan had already picked his keys and wallet up off the desk. "Thanks," he said as he hurried out the door.

Roxy felt as if she was walking through a dream world when she left Michael's office. It was just routine, that's what he'd said. She needed to go out to the hospital on Route Twenty. He'd called over there while she was in his office and arranged for her to go in for a biopsy—just like that! No waiting for an appointment, nothing. That probably worried her more than anything. Whenever she'd had to go for medical procedures in the city, it'd taken at least a week before she even heard anything.

"Are you okay?"

She turned to see Abbie sitting behind the reception desk, looking concerned.

"I think so."

"That doesn't sound good."

Roxy looked around the waiting room. It was empty. She looked back at Abbie. "Is it normal for him to send someone straight from here to the hospital for tests?"

Abbie smiled. "It is. It surprised me, too, when I started working here. I didn't think things would go so quickly. But since it's a rural hospital, they're not overwhelmed and understaffed like most are. We're lucky, I guess."

Roxy forced herself to smile. "That's good."

"Are you sure? You look a bit pale."

Roxy sucked in a deep breath and straightened her shoulders. "I'm fine. I just need to go and get these tests out of the way so I can get back to work." She didn't know Abbie that well, but it struck her that she hardly ever saw her out. "Are you doing anything on Thursday night? You should come out for dinner. A bunch of us girls meet up most weeks. You should join us."

Abbie smiled. "That's sweet of you. Thank you. I might just do that."

Roxy nodded. "You've got my number. Send me yours so I can call and remind you."

"Thanks.

They both turned as an elderly couple came in. Roxy rushed to hold the door open for them and then let herself out once they were safely inside.

She walked back around the side of the building to the little parking lot in the back. She frowned when she saw a very familiar truck parked next to her car.

She couldn't help smiling when Logan climbed out of the cab and gave her a shamefaced look.

"Don't be mad at me?"

She laughed and hurried to him. He wrapped his arms around her, and to her surprise, once she felt his solid, comforting presence, she burst into tears.

He held her tighter and kissed the top of her head. "What did he say?"

"Jeez! I'm sorry. I didn't mean to bawl at you. He didn't say there's anything wrong with me at all. He just said he wants me to get it tested to see what it is."

"A biopsy?"

"Yeah. See, even you know that's the next step. It's standard procedure, just to get it checked out."

He nodded, but she could tell by the look in his eyes that he was more worried even than she was.

She wiped her eyes and made herself smile. "I should be mad at you. I told you I didn't want you to come."

He shrugged and gave her a half smile. "You only said that you didn't want me to go with you. You didn't tell me not to come."

She laughed. "Hmm. I did. And to be fair, I'm really glad you're here."

"You are?"

She nodded and nestled closer against his chest. "I thought I was fine. I didn't think I was worried at all. But when Michael said I have to go straight to the hospital, I was kind of in shock. And me turning on the waterworks like I just did says that I might be a teeny bit worried."

He dropped a kiss on top of her head. "That's totally understandable. That's why I'm here. Do you want me to drive?"

She had to swallow the lump in her throat. She didn't even want to argue about him coming with her. Instead, she nodded gratefully. "Yes, please."

Chapter Nineteen

Roxy tried to stay as busy as she possibly could for the rest of the week. When her mind wasn't occupied, it kept sneaking back to the scary possibilities—the what-ifs. She couldn't afford to go there. She was a practical kind of girl—she prided herself on that. She didn't spend time worrying about anything normally. Her philosophy was that if things went wrong, she'd deal with them when they did. Until they did, there was no point in putting time and effort into things that might not even happen. That was easier said than done right now. This could be a very big something to go wrong for her. She didn't know what kind of treatment she'd need if it turned out to be … the worst news.

By Thursday afternoon, she was feeling frazzled as she drove home from work. She was supposed to be going out with the girls tonight. She really shouldn't cry off, since she'd invited Abbie to join them.

Her phone rang, and she pressed the button on the steering wheel to answer, expecting it to be Logan. He'd had to drive down to the city today. She knew he usually stayed overnight when he went, but he'd insisted that he'd come home.

"Hi, Roxy. It's Mom!"

"Oh! Hi!" Her heart raced. Her first thought was that she didn't want to worry her mom until—unless—it was necessary. "How are you?"

"Everything's fine here. I'm good. Ged sends his love. So does your brother. You should give him a call sometime. It'd be nice if the two of you talked more instead of sending messages through me."

Roxy smiled. "You're right. We haven't had a chat in a while. I might give him a call at the weekend."

"You'll be too busy this weekend."

"I will? Why?" Her heart sank. She had a feeling she knew the answer.

She was right. "We're coming to see you. And don't worry. You don't need to dash home and clean and tidy your house for us. We've already booked a room at the resort. That way we won't invade your space since it's such short notice. We wanted to surprise you."

"You did surprise me." Roxy wanted to cry. She loved her mom and Ged. They came and visited a couple of times a year, and sometimes they surprised her like this. They couldn't have picked a worse weekend, though.

"You don't sound very happy about it. Is it a bad time? Don't worry. I understand if you have other plans. We can entertain ourselves. The resort's lovely, and there's so much to do."

"No. It's not that." She pulled herself together. Hopefully, she'd get the all clear tomorrow and then it'd be great to see them. She couldn't wait to introduce Logan to them. She knew her mom would love him, and Ged would be all protective at first, but Logan would soon win him over.

"Is there anything you want to tell me?"

"What do you mean?" How could she know?

Her mom chuckled. "I've had this feeling for a while that you've got a new man in your life. Do you?"

"Oh!" She heaved a sigh of relief. "Yeah. I do. His name is Logan. You'll meet him at the weekend. I think you'll love him, Mom."

"I'll be the judge of that. Is it serious?"

"It's getting that way. You really will love him. He's so good to me."

"He'd better be."

Roxy laughed. "You talk tough, but I know you. Once you see how he is with me, you'll love him."

"I hope so."

"When are you coming?"

"Not until Saturday morning. I wanted to come tomorrow night, but Ged said we shouldn't hog both nights of your weekend."

"Okay. Well, call me and let me know what time you'll be here. It'll be good to see you."

"Will do. Is everything all right, Rox?"

"Of course, why?"

"I don't know, you sound funny, like there's something you're not telling me."

"Everything's fine, Mom, really." It wasn't a lie. As far as she knew right now, everything was fine. If she had … something wrong, she didn't know it herself yet, so there was no reason to go worrying her mom. "I'm a bit tired. It's been a long week already, and I'm just on my way home from work."

"You're driving? I'll let you go then. Are you seeing your Logan tonight?"

"I'm supposed to be going out for dinner with the girls." Again, not a lie. She hadn't said that yes, she would be seeing him both before she went out and when she got home.

"That's nice. Say hello to them for me and drive safely. I love you."

"Love you, Mom. Bye."

She gripped the steering wheel tighter. Please, please, let there be good news from the biopsy tomorrow. She couldn't stand the idea of having them here all weekend while she worried about it. She couldn't tell them, but it'd be a strain. Her mom knew her too well; she'd know that something was up.

~ ~ ~

Logan was surprised when he pulled into the driveway to see Roxy's car parked there. She was supposed to be out to dinner.

He smiled when he got out of the truck, and the front door opened. He usually came out when she arrived home and sometimes wondered if it was overkill, but seeing her standing there, bathed in the light from the hallway, did something weird to his insides. It melted them. It made him feel warm and happy and so glad to be home.

He bounded up the steps and wrapped her in a hug. "I missed you."

She chuckled. "What since this morning?"

"Yeah. I've been all the way to LA and back since then."

"Well, you're home now, and I made us some dinner."

"I thought you were going out for dinner?"

She shrugged. "I didn't feel up to it. I can't focus. I'm just so impatient to get the all clear tomorrow."

He hugged her closer. Hoping that she was right—that it would be good news. "That's what I want, too, but remember, they didn't say it'll definitely be tomorrow. Only that straightforward cases take two or three days."

She scowled at him. "And I've been good. I didn't get my hopes up that I'd hear today. Tomorrow is three days."

He led her inside and closed the door behind them. Not wanting to remind her that the folks at the hospital had said that sometimes it could take seven to ten days. "I know. But even if we don't hear tomorrow, we can do something fun this weekend—something to take our minds off it until we do."

He took his coat off and hung it on the back of one of the stools in the kitchen. "What did you make? It smells great."

The expression on her face worried him. "What? Did you hear already? Is it bad news?"

"No!" She shook her head rapidly. "It's just when you said about doing something fun this weekend. I'm not sure how fun you'll think this is, but my mom and Ged are coming."

"Did you tell them? Are they worried?"

"No, I didn't. And even if I haven't heard anything, I don't plan to tell them. I don't see the point in worrying them if I don't have to."

He nodded. He could see her reasoning, but he knew that would put a strain on things. He frowned. "Have you even told them about me? That you're living with me?"

She made a face. "I told Mom about you on the phone tonight. I didn't say that I'm staying here, just that they'd get to meet you—and they'd love you."

He blew out a big sigh and went to her. Resting his hands on her shoulders, he looked down into her eyes. "You're only staying here?"

She smiled as she looked up into his eyes. "I think I am. I mean. I've slept here every night since we started seeing each other."

He gave her a stern look. "If that's how you see it, then there's something I need to ask you?"

She looked worried. "What?"

"Do you want to live with me? Permanently."

His heart raced, wondering if he'd been assuming too much this whole time. As far as he was concerned, she already lived with him. She wasn't just *staying* here.

He relaxed when she grinned. "Yes. I do want to. I just didn't want to say it out loud in case it scared you."

He placed his hands around her waist and lifted her up to sit on the stool. Then he stood between her legs and curled his arms around her waist. "For such a smart woman, you can be pretty dumb sometimes."

She opened her mouth in an indignant huff, but he put his finger over her lips. "Let me explain. You think that you wanting to live with me might scare me? You haven't noticed this last week that the thing that scares me most in the world is the thought of something happening to you—of losing you?"

He had to swallow around the lump in his throat and blink away the tears that were pricking in his eyes. "I can't imagine living without you anymore, Rox. I know we've not been together that long, but even before we got into this, I knew you were someone I respect and admire. Now I know that I love you with all my heart and soul. You're everything." He shook his head. "Sorry if this sounds sappy as shit. I can't help it. I need you to know. I need you to understand. When I said you're my person, I meant it. You're the person I want to spend the rest of my life with."

Her eyes were round with shock. Maybe he should have waited. Maybe it was too soon, but with all the stress of this week, he'd figured out how he felt in a hurry. Nate had stopped by his office the day after her appointment. He'd seemed worried that Logan might feel under pressure to have to take care of her if it were bad news. That thought hadn't even occurred to him. All he wanted was to know what he could do to take care of her. To be there for her. To see her through it and support her. He'd bitten Nate's head off when he asked. But Nate had just laughed and said he'd been curious how serious things were between them—he had his answer.

He held his breath while he waited for her to speak. Maybe she was going to tell him that he was going too fast—or worse.

One fat tear rolled down her cheek, and he braced himself for the worst.

"You're an amazing man, Logan Perkins, and I would love for us to be together—for good. But if this does turn out to be bad news, it wouldn't be fair to ask you to stick around. I wouldn't do that to you. It wouldn't be fair. I love you too much."

He couldn't help it; a tear escaped his own eye. "You don't have a choice. You just told me that you love me and that you want me. You're not getting rid of me. What wouldn't be fair would be not letting me support you through this—if it even turns out to be what we think."

He took a deep breath. He was about to utter a word he hadn't thought he'd ever use. "One day, you're going to marry me."

He felt her body shake and realized she was laughing.

"I'm not kidding!"

Tears streamed down her face. "I know! I just can't believe you said that—and that you meant it! I know you meant it. And …" She wiped her eyes before looking back up at him. "I think you're probably right."

He lowered his head to hers and captured her lips in a kiss that he hoped told her more than he could manage in words. He was shocked at himself. He hadn't thought he was the marrying kind, but he did now. She made him want to be the best man he could be for her, to go through the best and the worst parts of life by her side and face them together. Especially that in sickness and in health part.

Chapter Twenty

Roxy was on edge on Saturday morning. She sat at the island in the kitchen, sipping her coffee. Logan was in the shower. He knew she liked to drink her first cup in peace even on the best of days. Today certainly wasn't the best. She hadn't heard anything from the hospital yesterday. She'd called, and they'd said that the results weren't back yet. She'd hear just as soon as they heard. Not only was it torture to have to go through the whole weekend with a cloud of dread hanging over her, but she was also going to have to act upbeat and happy for her mom and Ged.

She hoped that if she could get enough caffeine in her, she could pull off a bright and breezy façade that they wouldn't see through. Maybe she could kill two birds with one stone; get so distracted by putting on an act that she'd be able to take her mind off it. Somehow, though, she doubted it.

She took another sip of coffee and then sat up and forced herself to smile. She knew that you couldn't hold negative thoughts in your mind at the same time you held positive ones. And if she could just pull herself together, she knew she had a lot to be positive about. She looked around. She lived here!

Here with Logan. Sexy, supportive Logan. Logan, who had told her that she was going to marry him one day. Her smile was more genuine now. Strange as it might seem—crazy as it would have sounded not much more than a month ago, she believed he was right. Like he'd said, they'd known each other for a few years now. It wasn't like they'd just met. There was no rush, it wasn't like she was in a hurry, but just knowing that he felt that way—that he saw her as his person—made her happy. She believed in him. She believed in their future.

Her phone rang, bringing her back from her happy musings about what their wedding might be like someday.

"Hi, Mom, where are you?" she forced herself to sound bright and breezy.

"We're about an hour out. Should we come straight to your place, it's too early to check into our room."

Roxy's heart raced. Crap! She hadn't even thought! They didn't know she was here. Didn't know that she lived *here*! She took a deep breath. She might as well clear it up right now. That would be better than trying to hide it. She was trying to keep one thing secret from them already this weekend, but that was only so they wouldn't worry.

"Err … I should have told you. I haven't been spending much time at my house lately."

"Logan? Are you living with him?"

She almost said *kind of* as if that might make it more acceptable, less of a shock, but she made herself be honest. "Yes. I know you might not approve …"

Her mom sighed. "I'm not thrilled. We haven't even met him."

"I promise you, Mom. When you meet him, you'll understand just why I love him so much. We're not just shacking up. This is it. We're serious, we're starting our future together." She looked up to see Logan leaning in the doorway with a towel wrapped around his waist. The smile on his face made her glad that she'd decided to be upfront about it. Now, not only could her mom have no doubts about how serious she was, Logan couldn't either.

"Like I said, I'm not thrilled, but I'll try to reserve judgment until the weekend is over. So, what's the address? Are we coming to his house, or would you rather meet us somewhere?"

She looked up at Logan, hoping he wouldn't mind. "I can give you the address if you want to come straight here?"

She was relieved when he grinned and nodded. He'd said he was eager to meet them and get to know them. She was glad he didn't mind having to do that in his own home.

After she gave her mom the address, she hung up and held her arms out to him. "I need a hug."

He came straight to her and dropped a kiss on her lips as he closed his arms around her. "Are you okay?"

She nodded against his still damp chest, wishing they could go back to bed. "I'm fine. I just wish they'd wanted to come next weekend."

She felt him nod, but she knew what he was thinking— maybe by next weekend, she'd only have bad news to tell them.

Logan took a deep breath when the doorbell rang. He enjoyed meeting new people, but these were very important people. He hoped they were going to like him. It didn't help that he knew he was hiding something from them. It was

Roxy's right not to tell them about the lump and the biopsy if that was what she chose. But he didn't like feeling that he knew something that they didn't—and was hiding it from them.

She came and took hold of his hand. "Are you ready for this?"

He grinned and led her to the door. "Of course, I am. They're going to love me!" That was usually his attitude toward new people. And although his confidence wasn't quite as robust today, the way Roxy rolled her eyes at him before she opened the door told him that he'd convinced her.

"Roxy!" Her mom stepped forward and hugged her.

Logan had to smile. They said that if you wanted to know what a woman would look like when she got older, you had to see her mother. If it was true, then Roxy would look great.

He smiled at the guy standing by her side, who held out his hand. "Hi. I'm Ged. Nice to meet you."

"You, too. I'm Logan. Come on in."

Roxy's mom finally let go of her and gave him a warm smile. "I'm Janet." She held her arms out. "And I'm a hugger."

Logan laughed and leaned in for a hug. "I'm a hugger, too."

"Put him down, Mom," said Roxy. "Come inside. It's freezing out here."

"It is," agreed Ged. "We saw snow on the way here."

"Oh, Mom! You'd love where we went last weekend. Stanton Falls. It's this cute little town and it's all done up for Christmas already and they had loads of snow."

"That sounds lovely," said her mom. "I'd love to see that."

Logan raised an eyebrow at Roxy. "We could take a drive up there tomorrow," he suggested.

Ged smiled at him. "Way to win over the prospective mother-in-law. If you take her Christmas shopping, she'll love you forever."

Logan chuckled. "Like mother, like daughter then?"

"Yep." Roxy and her mom both grinned at him.

He looked at Ged. "I'm guessing you wouldn't want to get in the way of some serious shopping any more than I would. It might work out if we sit and drink hot chocolate and leave them to it."

Ged grasped his shoulder with a grin. "I like you already."

Logan discovered that he liked Ged right back. Roxy made everyone hot drinks, and they sat in the living room and chatted. It was easy conversation. They were curious about him—understandably—and wanted to know about his background and what he did. The last time he'd met a girl's parents had been quite a few years back. He'd felt inadequate somehow when he'd told them he worked construction. Now he was proud to tell them that he was the site manager at a major housing development on the other side of the lake.

Roxy's mom looked at her watch. "Where's the time gone? We've sat here yacking for a couple of hours. We should go and get checked in."

"Do you want some lunch first?" asked Logan.

Roxy made a face at him.

"We could have lunch at the resort," he added hurriedly. He hadn't meant that she should make them something.

She nodded. "Yeah, do you want to do that?"

"Sure," said Ged. "We'll follow you over there. I got a bit turned around on the way here."

"If you used GPS, it tries to take you the long way around town. You'll see how straightforward it is now." Logan smiled at him. "Then you'll know how to get here in the future."

~ ~ ~

Roxy would have liked to sit outside on the deck of the Boathouse for lunch, but it was way too cold for that. Instead, they found a booth inside.

She was pleased how well Logan was getting along with her mom and Ged. Her mom had shot her a few approving glances already. Roxy had known that she'd like him.

She didn't look very approving right now, though. She was giving Roxy a look she didn't understand.

"What's up?"

Her mom frowned. "I don't think I want to say."

"Why not?" Her mom wasn't usually backward about coming forward.

"Go on. You might as well say it as have us all sitting here wondering what the secret is." Ged winked at Roxy.

Her mom shook her head. "That's what I want to know. What is the secret?"

Roxy's heart raced. She'd thought she was doing so well. "What secret?"

"Whatever it is that has you so on edge. And has Logan constantly checking that you're okay." She smiled at Logan. "I'm sorry. I can't help but notice that you're super protective. If it was just you, then I'd think it's just your personality. But Roxy here is doing such a good job of being a little ray of sunshine that I know she must be hiding something."

Roxy's heart sank. She should have known her mom would see straight through her. She glanced at Logan. He looked as panicked as she felt. He'd suggested that they shouldn't hide what was going on, but she'd been adamant. She didn't want to worry them.

Her mom met her gaze directly. "Are you pregnant?"

Roxy laughed out loud at that. It was ridiculous. And so far from the truth. "No. I'm not."

Her mom looked at Logan. "Then, will you please tell me what's going on?"

Logan turned a pleading look on Roxy. It wasn't fair to put him in that situation, and Roxy knew it.

"It's not his to tell," she said. She blew out a big sigh. "And I'm probably being stupid, probably making something out of nothing. But I didn't want to worry you."

"About what?" Both her mom and Ged looked worried now.

"It's probably nothing. We'll probably laugh afterward about how dumb we were to make such a big deal out of it."

"Roxy! Just tell me!"

She swallowed. "I went to the doctor this week, and they sent me for some tests. I'm waiting for the results."

Her mom had turned white. "What kind of tests? What for?"

"I have this little lump."

"In your breast?"

She nodded.

Her mom's hand came up to cover her mouth. "You had a biopsy?"

Roxy nodded again.

"When will you get the results?" asked Ged.

"I was hoping that they'd come back yesterday. But probably Monday now. I'm sure it'll all be fine. Most lumps are benign. The doctor told me that."

Her mom visibly pulled herself together. "Yes. I'm sure it'll be nothing. I wish you'd told me sooner."

Roxy shrugged. "I didn't want to worry you—and to be honest, I've been trying not to think about it. I just want to get the all clear and put it behind me."

Ged looked at Logan. "I imagine it's not been the easiest week for you? And then we land on you, unexpectedly."

Logan shrugged. "I'm glad to meet you. But yeah, it's not been easy, and Roxy really just didn't want to worry you. We were hoping that she could tell you about it afterward."

Roxy could tell by the way her mom was watching him that she was weighing him up more carefully.

"You know I will worry." Her mom turned back to her. "But even if it turns out to be cancerous. You can always come home. We can take care of you."

"Thanks, Mom." She glanced at Logan. She didn't want to think about worst-case scenario. She'd deal with that when it happened. But that man sitting right there had already made it clear to her that he'd be by her side no matter what. She loved her mom, but Logan was the one she wanted to face this with. She reigned herself in. That was only if she had to face anything. She had to keep believing the results would be good.

Logan wasn't surprised when Janet asked if she could steal Roxy for a while after lunch. He understood that she'd want some time alone with her daughter. He'd expect it under any circumstances, but especially after what she'd just heard. He was surprised, however, that Ged asked if he wanted to hang with him while the girls did their thing.

He offered to take him for a drive around the lake, thinking that he might not have been over to the east shore. Of course, he had. They'd been over to the Lodge to see where Roxy worked.

"I wouldn't mind seeing this housing development of yours, though," Ged said with a smile. "I knew they were building over there last time we came, but it'd be interesting to see. If you wouldn't mind going over to work on the weekend?"

Logan smiled back. "No, I love showing it off. It's great. I used to spend a lot of my Saturdays over there, so that's nothing new."

Once they were on the road, Ged glanced over at him. "You don't spend your Saturdays there anymore, or is it our fault that you're not there today?"

"No. Since Roxy and I got together, I only go in if she's working Saturday."

They rode in silence for a while. He could tell that Ged had something to say, but he decided it was best to just wait to see what it was.

Eventually, he blew out a sigh. "I'm not good at beating around the bush. So I'll just come out with it. If it's cancer, she's going to be in for a rough ride. If you're going to walk away, it'd be better for everyone if you do it now."

Logan pressed his lips together. He shouldn't be angry. Ged was only looking out for her. He waited until he knew he could speak calmly. "I'm not going anywhere."

"Sorry. I didn't think you were. But it needed to be said. I wouldn't think any less of you. It's a new relationship."

Logan banged his fist on the steering wheel. He couldn't help it. "We've not been seeing each other that long, but we've been friends for years. I know who she is. I know I want her to be my wife."

Ged swung his head to look at him. "Your wife?"

Logan nodded grimly. "I hope you meant it when you said you like me already because I plan to be a part of your family."

To his relief, Ged smiled. "Does she feel the same way?"

"She says she does, but I think a part of her feels the same way you do. Part of her doesn't want to put me in a position where I'd have to support her—in every way."

"But you want to?"

"I do."

"Then can I suggest that you do your best to convince her of that before she gets the results. I don't know how you can do that, but you should try. If it's bad news, she might think she's doing what's best for you by walking away herself."

"I know." Logan smiled. "As a matter of fact. I have an idea. I'd like to run it by you; see what you think—see what her mom thinks."

"Lay it on me—I'm all ears."

Logan was relieved to tell him. It would also make it easier to explain one of the stops he planned to make over at Four Mile. He needed to visit one of the stores in the plaza.

Chapter Twenty-One

Roxy stared out the window of the truck as it wound its way up the two-lane highway into the mountains. She wished she could turn the clock back to last weekend. It'd been fun and light-hearted. Now her heart felt heavy. She wished she could just cling onto the idea that she didn't have cancer. But the fears and the what-ifs kept crowding into her mind. Logan said he'd be with her through whatever it took, whatever kind of surgery or treatment she needed, he'd be right there by her side. Her mom, on the other hand, had tried to convince her that she should move home. She didn't want to do that! But her mom had told her that if she needed chemotherapy, she wouldn't be able to live by herself, and it was too much to ask of Logan.

That last part had left her tossing and turning most of the night. He said he wanted to be there for her, but would it be fair to ask him?

He reached over and squeezed her hand briefly.

"It's so pretty up here," said her mom. "I love the snow."

Ged shuddered. "I don't mind looking at it, but only if it's sunny. Days like this are perfect. Bright blue sky. Lots of sunshine. I grew up in the northeast. And to me, snow means long cold gray days."

Roxy turned to smile at him. "I'm with you. I love it when the snow sparkles. It's like magic."

Logan squeezed her hand again. "I was thinking about what you said. Sunshine over snow is special. It takes something cold and hard and turns it into something sparkly and beautiful."

"Aww," her mom chimed in from the back. "Don't you have a way with words?"

Logan shrugged, and Roxy leaned over to plant a kiss on his cheek as he drove. "He's the best."

When they got to Stanton Falls, they parked in the same place they had last weekend. She looked at Logan. "Do you guys want to go do your thing? I won't subject you to the full shopping experience again."

He grinned at Ged who nodded happily.

"Yeah. Do you want to meet at the café at say, one?"

She looked at her mom, hoping that would be long enough.

"You can always go back for more after we have lunch," said Ged.

Her mom smiled, and Roxy got the idea that she and Ged had some secret of their own. "Don't worry. We'll be there at one o'clock on the dot."

Roxy kissed Logan, and her mom hugged Ged, then they went their separate ways.

"What do you think they'll do?" Roxy asked her mom. She felt a little guilty about leaving Logan with Ged again.

Her mom smiled. "I'm sure they'll find plenty to do. They had a good time together yesterday."

"Oh, good. Did Ged enjoy it, too, then? I know Logan enjoyed his company. He said they went over to the development."

Her mom gave her that sly smile again. "I'd say it was a great day."

"Are you two up to something? You keep grinning like a Cheshire cat."

"No! I'm just happy to be here with you. And happy that you've found yourself such a good man."

Roxy frowned. "I'm glad you like him. But what did he and Ged get up to yesterday? He sure seems to have won Ged over and I'm guessing Ged's convinced you, too?"

Her mom shrugged. "He's just a good guy. I can tell. I'm happy for you."

"Thanks."

~ ~ ~

Logan checked his watch.

"Relax. They've got ten minutes yet."

Logan grinned. "I can't help it. I'm excited, and I'm nervous. Even if she says no, I'm not giving up."

"I didn't for a minute think you would. This might only be laying the groundwork. It might just be what she needs to know that you're totally committed to her while she gets through whatever's going to happen."

Logan laughed. "Totally committed. Me. I don't exactly have the best track record, you know."

Ged shrugged. "That doesn't mean a thing. Neither did I when I met Janet. I was, what do you call it—a player? She had no reason to trust me. But I fell for her hook, line, and sinker. I changed my ways the minute I saw her. It happens."

Logan relaxed a little when he heard that. He knew that Ged had told Janet everything that they'd talked about yesterday, and she not only knew but was excited about his plan for today. He'd been concerned that she might be less enthusiastic about him when she learned how he'd been in the past. But it seemed that she, like her daughter, wasn't one to hold a man's past against him.

"Here they come."

Logan glanced over at the girls behind the counter and nodded. They were eager to help and seemed just about as excited as he felt.

He'd asked them if they'd bring out four hot chocolates a few minutes after Roxy and her mom sat down.

"Hey." She leaned down and kissed his cheek before taking off her coat and sitting down beside him.

"Hey. Did you have fun?"

She grinned. "That's a dumb question. I went Christmas shopping with my mom. We had a blast!"

Janet grinned at him. "Did you boys do what you needed to?"

He nodded. He was thrilled that she was supportive of this, but he wished that she didn't look quite so happy.

Roxy raised an eyebrow at him. "What did you need to do? Why do I get the feeling that everyone knows something I don't?"

"I don't know." He didn't want her to get suspicious now. He only had to get through another couple of minutes.

He glanced over to where two of the servers were standing smiling with the hot chocolates ready to come out. He nodded at them. He couldn't wait any longer.

"Oh, great! Thank you." Roxy smiled at the girl who set her hot chocolate down in front of her.

"I figured you'd want one of those."

Roxy nodded happily and looked down at the huge mug piled high with whipped cream and … a candy cane heart on top.

She put her hand over her heart and smiled at Logan. He must have asked them to do that. How sweet!

When he smiled back, his eyes were shiny. They were telling her that he loved her without him saying a word. She nodded, not wanting to share the moment with her mom and Ged. A quick glance told her that was a forlorn hope. They were both watching her, with big smiles on their faces.

"What's up?" she asked.

"Nothing." Her mom answered way too quickly.

"We're just happy to be here with you," said Ged. He plucked a candy cane from the rim of his own hot chocolate. "I know you love these things."

Roxy went to get one of hers; there were several of them hooked around the rim of the mug. She didn't want to eat the heart ones yet. She stopped, hand mid-air when she saw something shining on one of the canes. "What's that?"

She carefully picked it up and gasped when she saw a beautiful diamond ring taped to the little cane. "Oh, my God!" She looked at Logan, and he nodded and got up from his chair.

He bent down on one knee and took hold of her hand. "You know I love you, Roxy. But I don't think you know how much. It's going to take me the rest of my life to show you. Will you marry me?"

Her heart was thundering in her chest. Wasn't it too soon? What if she found out she had cancer?

She stared back into his eyes. He looked so hopeful; she felt so torn.

He untaped the ring from the cane. "I know you have doubts. I know you think I should have waited—and I can wait for you to marry me, we can have a long engagement if you want. But I need you to say that you want to marry me. That we're in this for keeps—no matter what life throws at us."

She looked at her mom and Ged. Ged was smiling, and she was surprised to see her mom nodding eagerly.

She looked back at Logan and nodded. If she said no, she'd break her own heart and his. She did want to spend her life with him. And if she did have a long, hard road ahead of her, she wanted to share that with him. "Yes!" she croaked. "I do. I will. I want to."

Tears ran down her cheeks as he slid the ring onto her finger.

"How did you know? I love this ring so much."

He chuckled. "Remind me where one of your best friends works."

"Oh! Maria! The jewelry store."

"Yep. I swore her to secrecy, but I told her that if you said yes, we'd invite everyone over to celebrate."

She hoped that before the week was out, she'd have two things to celebrate. But even if this was the only one, she'd be happy. She'd face the other as it came.

Her mom and Ged hugged and congratulated them. The girls who worked in the café all crowded around to see the ring and tell her how lucky she was. She knew it—and not just about the ring.

When he woke up on Monday morning, Logan wrapped his arms around her and pulled her in close to him.

She smiled and planted a sleepy kiss on his lips. "We don't have time. And besides. I don't think I've recovered from last night yet."

"Don't worry. I haven't either. I just wanted to hold my fiancée on our first morning as an engaged couple."

He loved the way she held her hand up to admire the ring. "You done good, Mr. Perkins."

He laughed. "I know. I snagged you."

Her smile faded. "I just wish we knew if you're going to be in for a rough road."

"Maybe you'll hear today."

She nodded.

"You know you have to call me the second you do?"

"Of course. Though, if it's bad news, will they tell me over the phone?"

"I don't know. I think so. Do you want to take the day off? We could both call in."

To his surprise, she thought about it for a minute. "I'm tempted to, but no. If we do that, it almost guarantees that I won't get any news today."

He nodded. She was probably right.

He was in the shower when he heard her squeal. He almost broke his neck, running down the stairs dripping wet and naked. "What is it?"

She held up her phone. "That was Abbie. Apparently, the results were sent to Michael's office on Friday afternoon. There was some mix up; he didn't know they were going to him."

"And?" His heart felt as though it might beat out his chest. "You're clear?"

She nodded. Tears were rolling down her face. "It's benign."

"Oh, thank God." His hands were shaking as he cupped her face in his hands and kissed her.

She sniffed and wiped the sleeve of her robe over her face. "I probably shouldn't have been as freaked out as I was."

"How could you not be? The man who loves you was losing his mind with worry."

"I scared Mom and Ged for nothing, too. I should call them. Let them know."

He smiled knowing how relieved they'd be. "How do you feel about calling in and asking for the day off now?"

She nodded. "I'll call Angel after I call them. Do you think you can?"

"Nate will understand."

"Are we going back to Stanton Falls?" asked Roxy when they'd been on the road for a while.

"Not quite. We're nearly at the spot I want to show you." He turned off the highway a few minutes later and followed a gravel road up to a trailhead he used to come to as a kid. There wasn't much snow on the ground here, but it still sparkled in the sun. That was all he needed.

They got out and walked up a little way to a bench that overlooked the valley. Roxy leaned against him, and he wrapped his arm around her shoulders.

"Sunshine over snow."

She looked up at him. "Is that why we came here?"

He nodded. "I know you love it. I know it makes you feel good. Today we had some magic happen for us. I need you to know that whenever snow falls in our lives—whatever goes wrong for us—I'm going to do my best to be like the sunshine for you. I'll try to shine and be your warmth so that you don't notice how cold and hard life can be. You deserve sparkles and magic."

"Aww!" She put her hands on his shoulders and reached up to kiss his lips. "You're not Logan Perkins ladies' man anymore. You're Logan Perkins, heart of gold and soul of a poet. And I'm the lucky one who gets to be with you. I love you."

"I love you, too, Rox. I don't know about the poet thing, but I do know I'm Logan Perkins, Roxy's man. Forever." ;

;

A Note from SJ

I hope you enjoyed Logan and Roxy's story. Please let your friends know about the books if you feel they would enjoy them as well. It would be wonderful if you would leave me a review, I'd very much appreciate it.

Check out the "Also By" page to see if any of my other series appeal to you – I have a couple of ebook freebie series starters, too, so you can take them for a test drive.

There are a few options to keep up with me and my imaginary friends:

The best way is to Sign up for my Newsletter at my website www.SJMcCoy.com. Don't worry I won't bombard you! I'll let you know about upcoming releases, share a sneak peek or two and keep you in the loop for a couple of fun giveaways I have coming up :0)

You can join my readers group to chat about the books or like my Facebook Page www.facebook.com/authorsjmccoy

I occasionally attempt to say something in 140 characters or less(!) on Twitter

And I'm in the process of building a shiny new website at www.SJMcCoy.com

I love to hear from readers, so feel free to email me at SJ@SJMcCoy.com if you'd like. I'm better at that! :0)

I hope our paths will cross again soon. Until then, take care, and thanks for your support—you are the reason I write!

Love

SJ

PS Project Semicolon

You may have noticed that the final sentence of the story closed with a semi-colon. It isn't a typo. <u>Project Semi Colon</u> is a non-profit movement dedicated to presenting hope and love to those who are struggling with depression, suicide, addiction and self-injury. Project Semicolon exists to encourage, love and inspire. It's a movement I support with all my heart.

"A semicolon represents a sentence the author could have ended, but chose not to. The sentence is your life and the author is you." - Project Semicolon

This author started writing after her son was killed in a car crash. At the time I wanted my own story to be over, instead I chose to honour a promise to my son to write my 'silly stories' someday. I chose to escape into my fictional world. I know for many who struggle with depression, suicide can appear to be the only escape. The semicolon has become a symbol of support, and hopefully a reminder – Your story isn't over yet

Also by SJ McCoy

Summer Lake Silver
Clay and Marianne in Like Some Old Country Song
Seymour and Chris in A Dream Too Far

Summer Lake Seasons
Angel and Luke in Take These Broken Wings
Zack and Maria in Too Much Love to Hide

Summer Lake Series
Love Like You've Never Been Hurt (FREE in ebook form)
Work Like You Don't Need the Money
Dance Like Nobody's Watching
Fly Like You've Never Been Grounded
Laugh Like You've Never Cried
Sing Like Nobody's Listening
Smile Like You Mean It
The Wedding Dance
Chasing Tomorrow
Dream Like Nothing's Impossible
Ride Like You've Never Fallen
Live Like There's No Tomorrow
The Wedding Flight

Remington Ranch Series
Mason (FREE in ebook form) and also available as Audio
Shane
Carter
Beau
Four Weddings and a Vendetta

A Chance and a Hope
Chance is a guy with a whole lot of story to tell. He's part of the fabric of both Summer Lake and Remington Ranch. He needed three whole books to tell his own story.

Chance Encounter
Finding Hope
Give Hope a Chance

Love in Nashville
Autumn and Matt in Bring on the Night

The Davenports
Oscar
TJ
Reid

The Hamiltons
Cameron and Piper in Red wine and Roses
Chelsea and Grant in Champagne and Daisies
Mary Ellen and Antonio in Marsala and Magnolias
Marcos and Molly in Prosecco and Peonies
Coming Next
Grady

About the Author

I'm SJ, a coffee addict, lover of chocolate and drinker of good red wines. I'm a lost soul and a hopeless romantic. Reading and writing are necessary parts of who I am. Though perhaps not as necessary as coffee! I can drink coffee without writing, but I can't write without coffee.

I grew up loving romance novels, my first boyfriends were book boyfriends, but life intervened, as it tends to do, and I wandered down the paths of non-fiction for many years. My life changed completely a few years ago and I returned to Romance to find my escape.

I write 'Sweet n Steamy' stories because to me there is enough angst and darkness in real life. My favorite romances are happy escapes with a focus on fun, friendships and happily-ever-afters, just like the ones I write.

These days I live in beautiful Montana, the last best place. If I'm not reading or writing, you'll find me just down the road in the park - Yellowstone. I have deer, eagles and the occasional bear for company, and I like it that way :0)

Made in the USA
Middletown, DE
13 March 2020

86312569R00142